Abo _

Fiona McDonald was born in Nairobi, Kenya. She was educated abroad and in Scotland. She attended the Academy of Ballet, and qualified in dance, and became a teacher. She worked in Edinburgh and London, and in 1999, she started writing.

Her first book *Gunfire* was set in Texas.

The second was called *Katie Cameron,* set in Loiusiana and New Orleans.

Her third book, *The Abbey,* set on a Scottish Island. A short story called *The Reluctant Bridegroom.*

A^{THE}BBEY

AND

THE RELUCTANT BRIDEGROOM

FIONA MCDONALD

Matador
9 Priory Business Park,
Wistow Road, Kibworth Beauchamp,
Leicestershire. LE8 0RX
Tel: 0116 279 2299
Email: books@troubador.co.uk
Web: www.troubador.co.uk/matador
Twitter: @matadorbooks

ISBN 978 1785891 717

British Library Cataloguing in Publication Data.
A catalogue record for this book is available from the British Library.

Printed and bound by CPI Group (UK) Ltd, Croydon, CR0 4YY
Typeset in 11pt Minion Pro by Troubador Publishing Ltd, Leicester, UK

Matador is an imprint of Troubador Publishing Ltd

MIX
Paper from
responsible sources
FSC
www.fsc.org   FSC® C013604

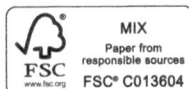

Acknowledgements

I would like to thank Mark Newman for helping with the manuscript of *The Abbey*.

I also would like to thank Newman Bates for the information regarding the Submarine.

I would like to thank Catherine Scotland for the manuscript of the *The Reluctant Bridegroom*.

The Abbey

Chapter One

The sun was shining brilliantly out of the cloudless sky, as Kathleen Robertson arrived at Glasgow's Central Station. She was looking forward to her holiday on the Isle of Risskay where her aunt and uncle lived. There was time for a coffee before boarding the next train to Oban. From there, she would catch the overnight steamer to her family's home. The coffee seemed to revive her after her trip from London's Euston Station to Glasgow, and as she gazed around, travellers seemed to rush for their various destinations. She hoped her brother John would arrive at the same time on the island, a place she had visited every summer except when she had been abroad.

The train left for Oban on time, and soon the scenery became dramatic with mountains and valleys, and although Kathleen loved this part of the journey, she soon fell asleep.

Her father Godfrey Robertson was born in Edinburgh in 1949 educated at George Watson School and had qualified as a chartered accountant. Juliet Rumsey, Kathleen's mother, was born in Edinburgh in 1950 and was educated at St Leonards School in St. Andrews, Fife. She became a secretary and met her husband while working in his office.

Godfrey and Juliet married, and in 1975 a son was

born. They named him John, and he also attended George Watson School like his father. He became a scientist.

In 1978, Kathleen was born and she was educated at St Leonards School like her mother. Kathleen was five feet five inches tall with brown hair and brown eyes.

Tragedy struck when Kathleen was fifteen. Her parents were killed in a car crash near Newcastle. John was at university at the time of their death, and Kathleen was at boarding school. She spent her holidays with her Mother's sister called Lucy Strachan. Lucy was a widow, and lived in Edinburgh.

John worked down in Southampton when he qualified, hardly returning to Scotland, although he kept in touch with Kathleen. Kathleen qualified as a secretary like her mother, and eventually went to London to work in an insurance company.

She hoped that 2000 was going to be a good year for her. She had a few boyfriends, but nothing very serious. All the boys her brother brought back when they were in their teens, had spotty faces, and they teased her.

The train arrived at the platform in Oban, a town situated on Scotland's west coast. Kathleen now prepared herself to board the *Pibroch* steamer, which would leave at approximately at 22.30 hours. One could book in early as there was a restaurant. Kathleen was shown her cabin which consisted of a bunk bed, toilet/hand-basin, and a view from a small window. She unpacked and changed in to a skirt and blouse, and made her way upstairs to the bar, where she had a gin and tonic. She was hungry, and glanced at the menu, and decided she would have a steak.

After the tedious long journey, she felt tired and so after dinner she was tucked up in bed and asleep. The next morning the boat was rocking, and she pulled back the curtains to find grey waves splashing against the boat. She was a good traveller but felt a bit light-headed. On deck it was very windy, and it was announced that the boat was three hours late due to the conditions. After breakfast, she hoped that her uncle would be there when they arrived on the island.

Three and half hours later the steamer approached Risskay. A small ferry boat made its way to the side of the ship to bring them ashore.

After a happy meeting with her uncle, Kathleen was glad to be on dry land, although she was a bit unsteady on her feet. They made their way to the car. The Land Rover proceeded its way past small lochs where men were fishing, and the vehicle passed up a driveway to a large white house, which over looked the sea, with glorious gardens.

Kathleen's Uncle Alastair Macnairn was a cousin to Godfrey Robertson. He was born in Edinburgh in 1940, stationed abroad in the army, and had retired to Risskay. He met his wife Hermoine in Edinburgh; she was born and brought up on the island. Alastair was sixty and Hermoine was five years younger.

Hermoine was a woman of five feet five inches, with grey hair and blue eyes. She and Alastair were not blessed with children, so she devoted herself to gardening, planting exotic flowers and plants.

Alastair was five feet nine inches tall, with a grey moustache, grey hair and a ruddy complexion. He loved to travel around the island visiting folk, especially the doctor, and they would discuss politics over glasses of whisky. He enjoyed having visitors and loved having John and Kathleen to stay during their holidays. He rarely went to the mainland, as he was tired of his travels around the world with the army.

Kathleen liked coming to visit her relatives ever since Aunt Lucy Strachan had died. She loved the peace and quiet of the island; nothing could be heard except the bleating of sheep from distant fields and farms. It was so different from London, where everyone was in hurry, and the summers so humid, so it was nice to get away.

She liked to sail and often went on Peter's boat, who was one of the local fishermen. She would also watch the boats return with mixed boxes of fish and would offer to help the men separate them.

Sam, the other Risskay fisherman, was married with three children, but his children had left the island to seek a more exciting lifestyle.

After a short rest and lunch, Kathleen went exploring the island on Hermione's bicycle, making her way down to the quayside where Peter and Sam had just come in from fishing.

Peter was a clean shaven, tall man with black curly hair and a wide smile. He had known Kathleen since she was a teenager, and he now looked forward to her coming to the island. He was single and lived beside the hotel with his dog Mag.

He looked up as Kathleen approached. "Good afternoon, Miss Kathleen. Good to see you back." he said.

Kathleen smiled and sat on the wall stroking Mag.

"Good to be back here once again, my brother is joining me this year, because it's difficult for him to get away from work." she said. Kathleen stood up, looked at her watch, then picked up the bicycle.

Peter said, "There is a Ceildh on Saturday in the village hall; I remember you liked to dance."

Kathleen replied, "Wonderful! You must surely give me a dance, Peter, and you too, Sam."

Peter grinned and wiped his nose on his sleeve. The seagulls circled the boat, diving into the water to catch the heads of the fish.

Kathleen made her way home after visiting the General Store, the only shop on the island. All the local folk were glad to see her back for her holidays, and were asking various questions about her life down in London.

Four days later, John arrived. Kathleen had not seen him since the scientific convention at the Savoy Hotel in London some months ago. They had always been close as children, but after their education, they had drifted apart.

On Saturday evening they all got ready for the Ceildh at the village hall. Alastair and Hermoine dressed in their evening wear, and Kathleen and John dressed casually. The hall was packed with people, and in one corner a bar was set up by Hamish Mackenzie, the owner of the hotel. Hamish was the third generation of his family who lived on the island, and he knew everyone and their business. He was a big man with a ruddy complexion and receding hair. He laughed a lot at his own jokes.

Everyone soon rallied around for the first dance which

was a Gay Gordon's. The band was on a small platform which consisted of a piano, fiddle and accordion. Kathleen danced the Gay Gordon's with her uncle, while Hermoine preferred to sit and watch.

John Robertson, Kathleen's brother, was just shy of six feet tall and had brown hair and blue eyes, except for teasing Kathleen, he was rather serious. He danced with one of the local lassies.

Kathleen went for a drink at the bar. She had danced three dances in a row and was now very thirsty. She turned around and came face to face with Colin Edwards. The last time she has seen him he was at the Savoy Hotel in London.

Colin Edwards was six feet tall. He had brown hair, blue eyes and a moustache. He worked with John in Southampton and was keen on Kathleen. Kathleen wondered what he was doing in Risskay; John had never mentioned that he would be coming. She found him attractive, but yet she was always rude to him; perhaps she did not want to truly show her feelings.

"What on earth are you doing here?" she said glaring at him.

He grinned and sipped his beer.

"You dance well, and you know your Scottish dances, so perhaps you could teach me," he said smiling at her. She was an attractive woman, and he remembered how they had met at the convention. She was beautifully dressed in a little black number, hair piled on top of her head. He looked at her now with her hair tied up in a ponytail. He was glad he had persuaded John to let him accompany him.

"John never mentioned that you were coming to the

island. Now that you are here, you can jolly well ask me to dance," she said, taking his hand and dragging him on to the floor.

Colin put his arm around her waist, and was thankful it was a waltz. He was not a bad dancer, but he did manage to step on her toes more than once. He looked into her eyes while they danced, and this made Kathleen feel rather embarrassed. The tempo quickened, and he guided her off the floor, as he did not want to continue.

As the evening progressed Colin got rather drunk, and had to be helped to his bed in the hotel by John. Kathleen asked her brother why had he brought Colin, but John just laughed and mentioned that Colin wanted to see her once again.

Kathleen was furious. How dare he bring him on her holiday, but secretly she was glad that he had.

Chapter Two

Kathleen came down to breakfast to find her uncle reading the daily newspaper. She helped herself to bacon and eggs, toast and tea before sitting down beside him. She was hungry after the dance the night before. She looked at him for a moment and then spoke.

"What are you doing today? May, I come with you if you are driving around the island?"

He looked over his newspaper at her, and drank from his cup. He said, "Today, I'll be looking over the estate. I noticed a fence broken down over on the north side; perhaps, it was a deer. You could come and join me, but I may need some help."

They made polite conversation for the rest of the breakfast and then got ready to leave.

Charlie, the spaniel, sat between them, as her uncle drove the Land Rover out of the gates of the estate. It was a lovely day, not a cloud in the sky, and Kathleen enjoyed looking at the countryside. They drove for a while, and then they passed two additional gates before making their way towards the woods. They parked the vehicle and walked towards the fence where the wire was bent towards the ground.

"Do you think that was made by a deer or a person?" She asked while flinging a stick for the dog to fetch.

Alastair looked at her and said, "What makes you think it was made by someone." He said looking at her.

"Oh just a thought," she said once again throwing the stick for the spaniel.

They mended the fence, returned to the car and drove home.

After lunch Kathleen helped her aunt in the garden. She enjoyed the fresh air, and wondered why she had not seen her brother or Colin. John had not appeared at breakfast or lunch, so perhaps they were suffering from hang-overs. Kathleen spoke, as she watched her aunt put some bulbs in to the earth. "It would be lovely to have a picnic at Lachlan Bay and a swim. What do you say, Auntie?"

Hermoine looked up and placed a hand on her back. "Mmm that would be a nice afternoon outing, not that Alastair or I could bear to go into the water. It is far too cold! We could ask Dr. MacNicol, his wife and daughter to join us. I will get Alastair to phone them later."

"Oh thanks, Auntie, I look forward to that very much indeed. We can discuss this at dinner tonight."

Kathleen was fed up with gardening and threw her gloves in to a nearby basket. She wanted to venture somewhere else.

Kathleen made her way down to the pier where Peter and Sam were sorting out the fish in to different boxes. She looked into the boxes, when a voice spoke.

"Interested in fish are we?" Colin said sitting down beside her on the wall. She glanced sideways at him.

"Feeling better now, are we? Fully recovered?" she said grinning at him.

Colin was dressed in brown cords, a yellow jumper, and he badly needed a shave. He turned to look at her. She was looking very attractive with her hair hanging loosely down her back. He knew she was mocking him.

"John has invited me up for dinner this evening. I saw him briefly earlier this afternoon," Colin said looking out to sea.

Kathleen wondered why Colin was here on holiday, and where was John? She had not seen him all day. She turned towards Colin. "Tomorrow we are possibly going to Lachlan Bay, and you are welcome to join us. We are discussing the details tonight after dinner." Colin wondered if she was being sarcastic.

"That would be great and yes, I can swim, dive for that matter and even walk," he said trying to keep a straight face.

She was beginning to get annoyed with him; he was poking fun at her. She turned to go, and saw John approaching them.

"Hi sis. Glad to see you are keeping Colin Company," said John while standing next to Colin.

She was getting annoyed with both of them, and she knew that John liked to tease her. She moved away from both of them and said, "I am going home now. See you both later." She marched up the slope not waiting to hear their comments.

Alastair and Hermoine always had cocktails before dinner every evening around 6.30 pm, and it didn't matter whether it was a gin and tonic, sherry or whisky. This gave

Mrs. Murray, the cook, time to leave the food on the hostess trolley before she left for home.

Kathleen wore a red dress, as her relatives always dressed for dinner in the evening, especially when they had guests. She looked at herself in the mirror, chose a red lipstick from her make-up bag, and applied it while taking care not to smudge her lips. She brushed her hair and stood up to give a twirl in front of the mirror. She came downstairs just as Colin was arriving, and their eyes met for a moment before they entered the lounge to join the others. Colin was dressed in a dark suit. His hair was neatly brushed back off his face, as it was usually all over the place. He had at least made an effort.

Kathleen brought up the subject of the picnic at Lachlan Bay and how it would be fun to spend the day there. Alastair informed them he had spoken to the doctor and his family, and they had agreed to come after the doctor had finished seeing patients that afternoon. The conversation then turned to the arrangement of the goodies and drinks to take to the bay, and who wanted to play games or go for a walk.

Alastair and Kathleen joined Hermoine in a game of cards. John and Colin stood by the French doors smoking. Suddenly, Charlie started to bark and run towards the hedge by the pond. A figure in dark clothing darted into the bushes before John could get a proper look. Colin followed the figure, but couldn't see anything, and whoever it was disappeared into the bushes.

Kathleen jumped out of her seat and immediately came towards the men.

"What is it; what's happening?" she asked her brother.

"Aye it's okay, sis; nothing to worry about. Probably some sheep that have lost their way," he said looking at her. It was best not to frighten her, but he had a good idea who it could be.

Kathleen wasn't sure what was going on between her brother and Colin or whether it some sort of game they were playing. The evening passed without any other incident, but Alastair mentioned that he would contact the local police to examine the hedge. John insisted that it was probably an animal.

The next day, they all set off for Lachlan Bay and met up with Dr. MacNicol and his family. The sun came out, and it became quite warm. They enjoyed the generous spread of boiled eggs, salad, cold meat, pies and sandwiches made up by Mrs. Murray and thermos flasks of tea and coffee.

Dr. James. MacNicol was a man his fifties with a bushy moustache. He was born in Inverness, attended the Academy, and qualified as a doctor after attending Edinburgh University.

His wife Freda was small with greying hair. She had been born on the island and was the local schoolteacher. They had a slightly handicapped daughter, called Lucy, who was seventeen years old. She adored the dog Charlie and was always hugging and stroking him.

Kathleen braved the cool waters of the Atlantic and shouted for her brother and Colin to join her. They did and splashed her with water, but Lucy just paddled at the water's edge.

Alastair and Hermoine spoke to the doctor and his wife. After Kathleen's swim was over, she suggested a walk, but the only one who joined her was Lucy, as the young girl knew the dog would be going. Kathleen loved the wind in her hair, and she and Lucy skipped along the path, while Charlie sniffed his surroundings. In the distance, two men were watching them through their binoculars.

Kathleen saw them and felt uneasy but reasoned that they could be tourists taking in the scenery. She called Lucy and the dog and retraced their steps back to the beach. They slid down the bank and spread sand all over the two women. Hermione was not amused.

"Careful! Watch what you are doing, you two! What's the hurry?" Hermoine said.

"Sorry, Auntie, we thought we would have a race back." replied Kathleen knowing she was telling a lie. They packed up as a cool breeze had started to blow. They were all tired and returned home for an early supper. Kathleen decided she would ask Peter the fisherman to take her out on his boat the next day, as she loved sailing.

She did mention to her brother about the incident with the two men at the beach. John just laughed and said they were probably tourists and that she had nothing to worry about. However, Kathleen was not convinced that John knew nothing at all. Why had somebody suddenly appeared at the house the other evening? It had never happened before…

Chapter Three

Kathleen stood at the bow of the boat feeling the wind on her face, and she felt free. She was really enjoying herself, as she leant over the rail to look at the rushing water. Peter was at the helm looking straight ahead, as he made his way towards the north part of the island. He had laid some lobster creels just off the coast near to where she had swum the other day.

She gazed north at the uninhabited island of Wisskay which had a ruined abbey on it. The locals said it was haunted. Many centuries ago, abbots and priests hid there from the Protestants who had hunted down and burned Catholics during the reign of Elizabeth the First.

The island fascinated Kathleen, and she wondered if Peter would sail around it. She looked at him and remarked, "Hey Peter, can we go over to the island of Wisskay, not to land but to sail around it?"

"What's so interesting on the island?" he replied, as he collected the lobster creels.

Kathleen shrugged her shoulders and gave him a smile. "I wanted to have a look at the abbey. I know it is a ruin, but there could be some interesting wildlife," she said coming towards him.

Peter placed the creels full of lobsters at the stern of the boat and looked up at her. Poor lass, she was on holiday here, so he might as well please her. "Okay, I have to get some more lobsters, and then I will take you over there," he said starting up the engine again.

The island of Wisskay was situated north of Risskay, and the ruined abbey was on the south side of the island where overgrown grass and moss surrounded it. The island was not very big, and on the west side, there were quicksands. There was also a lighthouse at the northern tip.

It was late afternoon when they returned, and she thanked Peter for an enjoyable trip. She mounted the bicycle and made her way home. She stopped for a rest beside a loch and looked around her. Everything was so peaceful, but then a light shone flickering off and on, and it appeared to be coming from the other side of the loch. She ducked behind a big bush and blinked several times. Was she dreaming this or was somebody signalling?

She continued her journey home and got ready for the evening. She was going to mention her day trip as well as the mystery signalling.

Colin Edwards was once again at dinner and discussed how he and John had gone over to the west of the island for a day's hiking. John was rather interested in keeping fit while he was here, as he had no time when he was working down south. They asked Kathleen how her day was. She told them about her very good time at sea, but also mentioned the strange appearance of the light signals at the loch side, and asked them what they thought it might have been. John told her it was probably some tourists getting lost, but once again, Kathleen did not believe his explanation. There was something strange happening: the two men on the cliff top, the disturbance at the hedge by the house, and now the flickering lights.

Kathleen was tired, so she excused herself from the present company and went up to bed. She sat and gazed out of the window, while she listened to the sheep bleating in the far away fields. She also wondered what she would do the next day.

Kathleen was up early the following morning and decided to investigate more of the island by bicycle. There had been no sign of her brother, uncle or aunt at breakfast, but she wanted to be alone for a while. It had started to rain while she was cycling, so she found an old ruined croft and tried to shelter as best as she could without getting too wet.

She heard a commotion coming from up on the hillside, and she peeped around the corner of the croft to see what was happening. Someone was coming very fast towards the building, so she looked around to see if she could find a stick to defend herself. The sound was coming nearer; she lifted a thick branch from a nearby tree and raised it above her head. She was feeling very nervous and frightened and wondered if she was being followed.

She struck out and hit the approaching man over the head with the thick branch. He fell to the ground in pain.

"What the hell!" he groaned holding on to his head. He glanced up at her, and she saw that it was Colin.

"What are you doing by rushing down a hillside and giving me a fright!" she said rather annoyed.

"I was following you, just in case you got into some sort

of trouble," he explained whilst brushing off leaves from his jacket.

"What do you mean by *following me*? What does that mean? I could look after myself even before you came on the scene," she said wheeling the bike and pretending as if she was leaving.

"Your brother thought it best to keep an eye on you. Just in case," he said staring at her.

"What do you mean *just in case*? What is going on Colin; there must be something you are not telling me," she said tossing her head back and looking straight at him.

He looked at her and wondered if he should tell her what her brother wanted? No, better not. Not yet. He wanted to kiss her, but he would probably get his face slapped. "Look, why don't we go to the tearoom in the village and have some tea or coffee," he offered. He did not want her to go; he wanted to get to know her. She looked at him and thought why not; perhaps he would tell her what was really going on.

They walked back down the road making polite conversation, and as it was still raining, they both looked forward to get something warming to drink.

They sat in a corner of the tearoom; there were only one or two couples in the room, and they paid no attention to them. Kathleen thought it may be wise to get to know Colin; after all he was not a bad guy, just a bit of a pain in the neck. They ordered two coffees and two scones, and Kathleen began to feel quite peckish; it was a while since she had breakfast.

They talked about their work and then Kathleen asked,

"Why did you come to the island with John? He's never brought anybody else with him on holiday? So why now?" she asked sipping her coffee.

He looked at her before replying. "Well I have never been to Scotland before, and John thought it would be a good idea for me to come and visit the island. He never mentioned that you would be coming. It is different from the big cities, and I am enjoying it very much indeed. I am also enjoying your company," he explained with a smile.

Kathleen thought for a moment. Surely this was not the real reason he was here. There was something not quite right, and she was going to find out what was at the bottom of all these mysterious happenings. Kathleen said goodbye to Colin, as he returned to the hotel. She made her way home hoping to find John so she could get some answers.

Alastair and Hermione were sitting in the conservatory reading the papers and were surprised to see her back so soon.

Kathleen sat down in the nearest chair and said, "Where is John? Have you seen him at all today? I want to speak with him."

Alastair put down his paper and looked at her. "He is upstairs in his room on the phone and has been for most of the morning."

"He should be out and enjoying the outdoors," replied Hermione.

Kathleen stood up and made her way up to John's room. He was still on the phone when her knock interrupted his call. Before he could say anything, Kathleen walked in.

"I want to talk to you now; I think you have been

avoiding me," she said sitting down on the nearest chair. He turned off his phone and looked at her. "I want to know what you and Colin are up to. I was sheltering at the old croft five miles away when a figure came running down the hillside, and as I have seen some strange happenings lately, I hit him over the head with a branch. This person turned out to be Colin. So why is he following me?" she said standing up.

John gave a laugh and said, "Oh, sis, you are silly! You know he is keen on you and wants to get to know you. There is nothing strange going on here."

Kathleen grunted but was still not convinced. She turned towards the window and gazed down at the garden below. "There are a lot of strange incidents occurring such as the figure in the hedge the other night, the two men on the cliff top and the signals at the loch. What does it all mean; can you explain this?"

John put an arm around her and said: "Come on, sis, it is all in your imagination; you have been reading too many detective books."

Kathleen looked at him. Was it her imagination? No, she was convinced that John knew something, and if he was not going to tell her, she would ask Colin. She made up her mind to be really nice to him.

Colin lay down on the top of the bed and gazed up at the ceiling. It was not in Kathleen's imagination. She had seen for herself that besides him following her, there were two other men keeping an eye on her brother. John had a plan for Kathleen, but he did not know what. Colin, however, wanted just to be near her just in case any harm came to her. He remembered her from the convention in London. She was stunning and had a good figure as well, especially her legs, and looked wonderful in her bathing costume the other day. If only she would relax more, he could draw her into his arms and kiss her. He fell asleep briefly dreaming of Kathleen.

Alastair and Hermione invited the MacNicol family and Colin for dinner that evening. Mrs. Murray had cooked homemade lentil soup, a roast lamb and an apple pie.

After dinner, they played whist, and Hermione played a tune on the piano. Lucy sat on a stool and stroked the dog. The men eventually talked politics and what was happening in general around the island. The ladies continued with their game of cards.

Colin lit a cigarette and moved into the garden in the hope that Kathleen would follow. John also joined Colin. Lucy ran after the dog into the garden, as Charlie investigated the various smells. Kathleen came out onto the terrace and walked down towards the pond. Lucy stood beside her, but her attention was on Charlie.

"Lucy, be a love and get my cardigan from the sitting room. It's getting rather cool," said Kathleen.

"Yes, of course," replied Lucy, running back into the house.

Kathleen moved further into the garden and away from the two men. She had just passed the pond when she suddenly felt someone grab hold of her and pull her towards the bushes. She screamed.

Colin came running towards her. She was crying with her arms around her body. "Help! Someone just tried to kidnap me," she said stammering. Colin put an arm around her shoulders to comfort her. John came down to see what was happening.

"What is it? What has happened?" John asked. Colin glared at John, but John ignored his look.

"Someone tried to pull me into the bushes. I do not know who it was, and it was so dark," she sobbed.

"Oh, dearie me. Sure it was not your imagination, sis?" said John taking her arm and making their way back to the house.

Kathleen was given a small glass of brandy to steady her nerves. She was pale, and her mascara had run down her face. "She will be alright after a good night's rest," said Dr. MacNicol.

"Perhaps it was a branch from a tree?" Alastair said.

"No, it was definitely not a branch of tree; it was someone dressed in black. Everything happened so quickly," said Kathleen crying again.

"Well, we better take our leave, as it is getting late. We'll look out for any ghosts on our way home," said the doctor.

Kathleen went to bed, while Colin approached John before leaving. "I do not like this; it is not her imagination. Did you arrange this to frighten her?" asked Colin.

John put his hands in his pockets. "Of course not. Why would I do a thing like that? She is my sister, for god's sake."

"Look, I just do not want to see her hurt," said Colin. John patted Colin on the back and pushed him out of the door.

John stood in the dark. His plans would now have to change.

Chapter Four

After the scare of the previous evening, Kathleen was delighted that Colin was accompanying her on her travels on the island. They had picnic lunches with them, as they knew it would be nearer teatime before they returned. They decided to walk up towards Bells Brae, and then, if they felt like it, they would climb the highest point of the island, which afforded views of Jura, Rhum, Eigg, Islay and Colonsay. It turned out to be a warm day, and Kathleen tied her sweater around her waist, so she had more movement whilst walking.

John had not joined them, as he was as usual on the telephone. He was keeping in touch with his work, as he had a busy schedule to keep up even whilst on holiday.

Kathleen was hungry, and she tucked into the cheese and tomato sandwiches Mrs. Murray had made. Afterwards, she reclined on the heather mound and gazed up into the sky. Colin lay near her, chewing a bit of grass whilst watching her. Neither spoke, as they both were enjoying the peace and quiet.

They made their way down towards the woods, as it was a shortcut down to the main road. Kathleen was walking slightly ahead of Colin, when he suddenly grabbed her and threw her face downwards. She struggled – what the hell was he doing?

"Shh, be quiet. Lie still and do not make a sound," he said as he lay sprawled over her. She could not breathe, as her face was lying in the heather. She struggled.

"What are you doing? You are crushing me. Get off!" she said struggling to get up.

There was the sound of footsteps cracking over the fallen twigs, and whoever it was, they were very close. Kathleen opened her mouth to speak, when Colin's hand slid over her mouth. Colin glanced up and saw two figures moving away; they were looking at the bushes, as if they were looking for someone or something. Colin was taking no chances.

"What are you doing?" she asked sitting up and looking at him.

He did not want to scare her, but he knew that these two men were looking for them. Colin helped Kathleen up, while she brushed off the heather and twigs attached to her clothing. "I am very sorry, but those two men were looking for something or someone, and I thought it best that we hid from them. I know there have been some strange happenings since you arrived on the island, but I am trying to work out what they want from you," he explained.

Kathleen looked at him, was it true that these people, whoever they were, were trying to kidnap her, but why? How did Colin know about this? Colin put an arm around her, and gave her a gentle squeeze to encourage her to be brave.

He said, "I will look after you; I promise. Please do not

worry. I am not sure what is happening, but I will protect you."

Kathleen bit her lip. She looked down before gazing at him. "What does this mean? I cannot enjoy myself on my holiday?" she replied gathering up her belongings, and moving downwards to the path leading to the road. Kathleen felt the tears fall down her face, she wanted to cry, but did not want Colin to know that she was really scared. She stopped and wiped her face with the back of her hand. Colin could see that she was upset. He took out a handkerchief, pulled her towards him, and wiped her tear stained face. After wiping her eyes, he tilted her face in his hand and pressed his lips on hers, at first very gently then with more pressure. Kathleen just stood there helpless. He was trying his best to cheer her up, and now he was kissing her. Why was she not protesting, or did she really want him to kiss her?

Colin thought it was best not to attend dinner that night; he wanted time to think, and instead, he made his way to the bar in the hotel.

Mr. Mackenzie poured him a pint of beer placing it in front of Colin. "Been a great day, cloudy mind, but no rain. Have you been investigating the island?" Mr. Mackenzie inquired.

The beer tasted good, and as Colin was very thirsty, he drunk it down in one. He nodded, as he placed the glass on the counter for a refill. "Yes, great day. Been walking among the hills and moors, and not a single soul in sight. Marvellous, just me and the odd sheep," he replied as he leaned with his back against the counter, while at the same time looking around to see if he recognised anyone.

The bar was pretty busy, and he recognised Peter and Sam, the fishermen, who were sitting in a corner with their pints of beer. He strolled over and asked if he could join them.

"Sit yourself down, lad. How are you enjoying your holiday?" asked Peter.

Colin drew up a stool and took a sip from his drink. "Yes, I went walking with Kathleen up on the hills over on the other side of the island," replied Colin. He did not want to ask too many questions regarding strangers, as they may wonder at the questions.

"Ah, yes, Kathleen, a bonnie lass, has always come to the island for her holidays since she was fifteen. Her parents were both killed in a car accident, and she spent her holidays with an aunt in Edinburgh, but I think she died also," said Peter sipping from his beer. He continued, "Where do you come from? London, is it? I went to Glasgow once, and never again; the crowds of folk all rushing about. Nay, that is not the life for me."

Colin laughed, and explained that he was from London but worked with John in Southampton.

A group of men entered the bar. Two were tall, while the other one was smaller. They ordered drinks and sat on the other side of the lounge. They kept together, not speaking to anyone, and ignored the rest of the folk in the bar. Colin wanted to have a good look at them and wondered if two of them were the ones who had followed them that afternoon. He tried to have a good look at them, but it became rather crowded, so he drank up and made his way to the restaurant.

Kathleen spoke to her brother about the episode in the woods, and how Colin had protected her. Why was someone so interested in following her everywhere she went? This had never happened before on her holidays on the island. Were they really after him?

John was silent as she spoke and never batted an eyelid. He knew that there was some truth that he could be in danger, because these men were after the highly secretive programme he was working on. He pulled his sister close and told her that she was not to worry. He would look into the matter.

Alastair and Hermione did not seem to worry about what was going on around them; they took every day as normal, Hermione doing her garden, and Alastair playing a game of golf or having a drink down at the hotel with the boys.

The next day Colin did not see the strangers, so he thought they were probably tourists, perhaps camping and just visiting the island, although the ferry only arrived twice a week. Many tourists came during the summer months which was good for the local businesses.

Peter and Sam were out fishing as usual and collecting their lobster creels, when a motor boat suddenly shot past their bow, spraying them with water. The two men looked at each other and at the boat as it sped off in the distance. It looked like it was making its way to the island of Wisskay, but nobody ever visited that island. People were too afraid of ghosts or fairy tales.

"Who was that? Do they not know the rules of sailing in these waters!" Peter shouted.

Sam rubbed his chin, and threw a box of fish towards the port side before replying, "Aye, these tourists have no idea of the ways of the sea. I hope they get stuck on that island; that will teach them."

Colin was sitting on the wall hoping that Kathleen would be in the village. He saw the two fishing boats coming through the harbour walls, and he wanted to have a chat with the two men. Colin waved at the two men and helped them tie up by the sea wall.

"Great catch you've landed," said Colin helping to unload the boxes of fish.

"How are you today? No sign of Kathleen or John," asked Peter.

"No, I have not seen either of them today, but I hope to see them later on this evening," Colin replied.

There was a moment's silence before Sam said, "We saw a speedboat making its way to the island of Wisskay. Nobody in their right mind goes over there. Nearly took our bows off with the speed they were going."

Colin thought that was interesting and asked, "How many folk did you see on this boat?"

Sam paused and said, "Three of them. One was at the helm and the other two were sitting and looking straight ahead. Why are you asking?"

"Oh, I saw some men drinking in the bar last night, and thought they were not like the other tourists I have seen so far on the island. I wondered what they were up to," said Colin. He was now resolved to take a boat out to investigate the island of Wisskay.

Colin said goodbye, and went to the General Store to see if he could find a book on Wisskay; if not, he would research it online.

Chapter Five

Kathleen got up early and had breakfast. Nobody was around, so she packed a bag with biscuits and scones, baked by Mrs. Murray, and set off down the road. It was good not to have anyone with her, and she felt free. She had not seen her brother or Colin since yesterday afternoon. It started to rain, and she pulled up the collar of her jacket and jammed her cap firmly down on her head. She walked swinging her arms, and eventually she came to a sandy beach. She slid down the sand to a rock and sat down. She placed her back firmly against the rock and gazed at the white waves bouncing along the water. Maybe she should not have come; a day like this one should be beside the fire, nice and cosy. She also knew that Colin and her brother would be cross with her for going out without telling anyone.

It started to rain quite heavily, and she slid further down into the sand, pulling her cap over her eyes. She began to think about why her brother and Colin were behaving so strangely. Was something terrible going to happen, and why did someone want to kidnap her? Maybe she should have left a note, but what was the use of that? She felt like a prisoner; after all, nothing like this holiday had happened before. Why was somebody watching her every move and was her brother involved? The seagulls circled the sky, calling out to the elements. They landed on the sea, where they bounced up and down. She felt hungry, so she ate one of the scones, while rubbing her hands together to get some life back into them. It was getting cold, and she shivered. She thought that perhaps she should get up and make her way back to the house.

She stood up and swung her arms to get some warmth into them before placing the bag over her shoulder and setting off toward the road. She decided to return near the woods, as one could get some shelter there. She strode out and left the road climbing the banking into the wood. The undergrowth crackled under her feet, and she gazed around her to see if anyone was following her. She continued and came to a clearing and wondered which way she should go. She climbed further up before stopping to get her breath back.

The view towards the sea was amazing. There were no boats, just the birds floating in the air with their wings spread out, as they balanced like acrobats moving up and down in the wind. She continued higher and higher up the worn path until she was on top of a hill. She could make out her house, so she knew she had not far to go. The path began to disappear, and she found it difficult to walk on the overgrown grass. She looked around her and nearly stumbled. Eventually, she decided to make her way down towards the road, as it would be easier to walk on that surface. She slid downwards nearly falling before catching herself on tree branches. Why did she come this way when it would have been much easier on the road?

She wondered if her brother or Colin had missed her yet. It must be lunchtime by now, and she looked at her watch and noticed that it had stopped. Maybe she should have taken Hermione's bicycle. It would have been quicker than this adventure. She heard someone coming, and she looked around to see where she could hide. She darted behind some bushes and held her breath while peeping through the leaves. A man was coming towards her. His hat was pulled down over his eyes, and he was concentrating on where he was going. He passed by her, and she waited for a few minutes before emerging from her hiding place.

She was becoming afraid, and she hurried towards the road. She came to a clearing. She could not remember if this was where she was before or if it was further back. She stood for a moment, and then suddenly felt something being placed over her nose and an arm grabbed her around her waist. She called out before collapsing.

The two men carried her down to the road and put her in the back of a Land Rover before placing a blanket over her. A tall, athletic, red-haired man sat behind the wheel, while the other smaller man sat beside him.

Kathleen woke up some time later and tried to sit up. She felt so dopey, and didn't know where she was. She could hear waves crashing against the rocks and the wind beginning to howl. There must be a storm brewing. She felt cold and groggy, so she closed her eyes and fell back to sleep.

The red-haired man, Alan Paterson, poured some whisky into a glass, and drank it down in one go. He had short hair and tattoos on his arms. He was from London and had left school when he was fourteen. When he was old enough, he joined the army and travelled abroad. He was in the SAS for a while and then joined a band of mercenaries, where he fought mostly in Africa. He was now in his forties and divorced. His wife had not taken to the life he led.

The smaller man was from Turkey, dark with a small moustache, and he also had been a guerrilla fighting in Africa, where he had met Alan. His name was Mouska, and he was separated and in his late thirties. He poured himself a cup of strong coffee and sat down looking at Alan.

"Now what happens? We have got the girl, so have you seen or been in touch with John?" he asked looking straight at Alan.

Alan wiped his mouth with the back of his hand, and looked at him. "I have not spoken to him since this morning. He told me that the woman had disappeared and to find her; then, he would be in touch again."

"So what do we do now? Just wait?" asked Mouska.

"Yes, we wait. Frank has gone shopping and will be back soon, as I think the weather is worsening," said Alan.

Kathleen woke again and lay listening to the storm outside. What had happened to her, and where was she? Was she dreaming? She remembered walking down the path and then nothing. Why could she not remember? A curtain was drawn back and a figure stood looking down at her.

"Where am I? And who are you? Why am I here?" she asked standing while gripping the blanket which covered her.

"Lie down and rest. Would you like some coffee?" the man asked.

"Yes, that would be appreciated. Where are John and Colin?"

The figure had already moved away. The coffee was strong but sweet, and she placed her hands around the mug to get her fingers warm. The room smelled musty and damp, and she looked around. There were books on a shelf and a small table and chair in the corner. The bed she was on was made of wood. Was this some sort of hide-out?

Frank Fletcher tied up the motor boat and lifted the groceries out. He made his way through the ruined abbey to the caves down below. He swung the shopping onto the large table and took off his jacket. "The weather is getting worse. We could be here for days unless it clears." He spied the bottle of whisky and poured himself a drink before sitting on a chair and looking at the other two men. "We have got the woman. She was at last alone, and we were watching from a distance to see where she would go," said Alan.

Frank Fletcher had long black hair down to his shoulders and a beard. He was Limerick born and had ventured over to England to find work when he was sixteen. He joined the army, and liked it so much that he was promoted to sergeant. But then he met Alan and joined the guerrillas in Africa.

Colin could not find Kathleen anywhere, so he rang the doorbell at the house. Hermione answered the door and let Colin in. He asked if John was about. She did not seem to be worried, and went back to sorting out her plant cuttings.

John looked up as Colin burst through the door.

"What have you done with her, and where is she?" said Colin. "Surely she has not been kidnapped."

John stood with his hands in his pockets. He turned and looked out of the window at the rain. "Yes, I am afraid that they have got her; I am awaiting instructions," he said.

Colin was angry. Why did she not wait for him? After all, they had agreed to investigate the Isle of Wisskay.

"You knew that if she went out on her own that they would kidnap her; why did you allow this?" Colin said placing his hands in his pockets. He wanted to hit John for being so careless. "What are these instructions? We have to get her back. If anything happens to her, I will never forgive you."

"Stop being so dramatic, you knew at the beginning what was going to happen. No harm will come to her, and anyway, she likes having an adventure; she told me so. I will get a lot of money if I sell my project; many countries are interested, and we are now waiting for Trevor to arrive on the island. In fact, I intend on going over to the island myself when the weather dies down."

"You mean you are going to leave her over there until Trevor turns up, but that could take days with the weather so stormy. You must go and get her as soon as possible. She has nothing to do with this operation," said Colin sitting down on the edge of the bed.

"You must be in love with her to go to all this trouble to rescue her. She is after all my sister," replied John.

Colin got up and closed the door. He could not wait any

longer, and Alastair and Hermione did not know anything about this. He had to get some help. He made his way down to the quay in the hope that Sam or Peter would be there to take him over to the isle of Wisskay.

Chapter Six

Kathleen woke to someone yelling, and she sat up and pulled back the blanket. She swung her legs over the bed and moved towards the voices. Three men were sipping coffee from their mugs, and the red headed guy was shouting. His arms were waving about, as he stood facing the other two. She was hungry, but still felt woozy from the drug they had given her. She moved forward to try to listen to their conversation.

"We are going to be on this damn island for weeks, and we still have not heard from Trevor or John. This damn storm. What I could do with is a pint of beer at the hotel. What about the woman? We can't keep her here for weeks," said Alan.

The men mumbled to themselves, and then realised that Kathleen was standing and staring at them. She smiled and said, "I could do with something to eat and drink. Would that be possible?"

Alan, the red-head, turned and looked at her, but Frank had already opened a loaf of bread, and had started buttering a slice or two. The kettle was put on once again for some tea or coffee. They indicated a chair at the table, and she moved forward and sat down looking from one to the other.

"Can you tell me why you kidnapped me, and why I am a prisoner?" she asked.

"We were to keep an eye on you, and we are now awaiting instructions," replied Frank, who was sitting down opposite her. She took a bite of her meagre breakfast.

"Has this to do with my brother's work?" she asked.

They looked from one to the other, and wondered how much she knew. Alan cleared his throat before speaking. "Now there is nothing to worry about. You will be released soon, but we have to wait until the storm blows itself out."

"I feel so tired, but thanks for the refreshment. I feel I have to go and rest once again." She rose from the chair and staggered forward towards the doorway. Frank guided her back to the bed, and she lay back and immediately fell asleep.

Colin moved down towards the quay, where all the boats were bobbing up and down in the water. He had to think of where they would have taken her. John was no use at all; he never really gave a straight answer. If he could get either Peter or Sam to take him to Wisskay, he would explore the island and maybe find Kathleen.

The crowd huddled together in the hotel bar; nearly every man on the island was there. The women folk were at home, while the wind was howling, and the door kept banging every time a customer came in.

Mr. Mackenzie was in his element telling jokes and pouring out the drinks, and, of course, spreading the latest gossip.

Colin sat in a corner clutching his drink, and looking to

see if there was anybody he knew. Peter was there with his dog, which was a bit scared of the crowds, and kept looking up in case someone stood on his tail. Colin made his way over.

"When do you think this storm will blow itself out? I am really worried, as Kathleen has disappeared, and I think she has been kidnapped. Have you seen John anywhere today?" asked Colin.

Peter stroked his chin and looked at Colin. "Kidnapped, you say? What do you mean, and who would do a thing like that?" replied Peter, lifting his pint to his lips. He continued, "No, I have not seen John. Funny bloke, keeps himself to himself. Hardly ever comes to the island on holiday, not like Kathleen. She is a fine lass." He took another swig from his glass. Colin stroked his head and took a drink.

"Look, as soon as the storm settles, could you take me to Wisskay? I would like to see if she is there. I will pay," said Colin.

Peter looked at him for a moment. "Nay need to pay me. I will take you, as this storm should have blown out by tomorrow. Anyway, I need to collect my lobster creels and do some fishing," said Peter. He finished his drink and stood up, tapped his forehead, and he and his dog made their way out.

Kathleen woke suddenly. There was dead silence, and she sat up and wondered what the time was. She could hear the waves hitting the shoreline. She swung her legs off the bed and looked into the large room where she had seen the men. There was nobody there. She made her way towards a dark passage. She needed some fresh air and that would clear her head. She moved very slowly, stopping to hear anything, but there was nothing. At last she felt a draught of air, and she inhaled it and moved quickly towards the exit. It was morning, and the wind still howled, and she could see the waves crashing against the rocks. There was a slight incline up a slope, and she moved up it to look around. Oh, where was John and Colin, and why was she not rescued?

John packed a small bag with some belongings and documents. He had received a phone call that all was ready and for him to come to the Isle of Wisskay immediately. He hoped that Kathleen was not too cross with him for arranging her kidnap, but she would be released soon.

Hermione wandered through the hallway carrying a tray of tea and cakes, as she made it to the lounge. Alastair was sitting reading the paper, and he looked up as she entered the room.

"Where is everybody today? There is no sign of Kathleen, and she never turned up for lunch. John does not say very much at all. I do not know what the younger generation is coming to," said Alastair.

"I have no idea. I have been too busy in the garden shed to worry what the young ones are getting up to," she said pouring out the tea.

"I think the storm is blowing itself out, so I will go down once again to the hotel and see what is happening before dinner time. You don't mind, love; do you?" he said sipping his tea and munching into an iced sponge cake.

Hermione shrugged her shoulders and smiled at her husband. She was used to his ways, and anyhow he enjoyed meeting the other boys, especially the doctor.

Kathleen stood on the banking and gazed around. She made her way towards the north of the island, where the lighthouse was situated. The waves were still very big and kept lashing against the rocks, and she had to be careful that she did not slip. She crawled along beside the water, while ensuring her footing was solid on the grassy verge. It was hard going, and her legs ached, as well as her arms. There might be a boat or dinghy somewhere hidden in a cove to allow her to escape back to the island. The grassy verge gave way, and she found herself on an overgrown path with ferns on each side which hid her from view. She fell two or three times, but she was eager to get to the lighthouse. There was no sound except for the gale-force wind and gulls crying out. At last she could see the lighthouse, and she stumbled along the rough terrain and fell into a shallow pool of water. To save herself, she put out her hand scraping it on a sharp piece of rock. It caused a deep cut to the palm of her hand. Blood streamed down her arm, so Kathleen felt in her jacket pocket for a handkerchief and found a tissue to tightly wrap it.

The wind was strong, and it took Kathleen a long time to get a few yards to the lighthouse. The lighthouse was locked, and she sat down with her back against the door and gazed ahead at the open waters. She heard the noise of a boat, and she stood up and looked around her. She could not see anything, but perhaps it was coming from the other side of the island. Someone was coming to save her; was it Colin? She hoped so, as somehow she always felt safe with him around.

Peter and Colin manoeuvred the fishing boat into the

small sandy cove on the island of Wisskay and tied up. Colin jumped ashore and ducked down by some rocks; he was not sure who was on the island, but he was being cautious. He felt in his jacket pocket and stroked his gun. He did not want to frighten Peter who stepped beside him.

"Maybe I should go fishing, and come back for you in an hour," Peter whispered into Colin's ear.

Colin turned and looked at him, and thought for a moment. "Yes, this could be dangerous, and if I am not here at this point, go back to the island and get some help," he said slapping Peter on the shoulder. Peter looked worried, but made his way back to the boat.

Colin watched as the boat backed away from the shoreline, and then proceeded up the slope towards the ruined abbey. He stopped every now and again to listen for a noise or voices, but the whole island seemed silent.

Kathleen decided to move, and she made her way towards where she thought the boat had come in. She was getting tired with the effort, and she felt cold and hungry. Had these men left her to die on this island? Where were they?

Colin moved silently down the slope and into the empty ruins of the abbey. He stood for a second and listened. Someone was coming, and so he slipped behind a pillar hoping that noone could see him. There were four men fast approaching the abbey each carrying boxes. Colin could see that it was John leading the group. He could not make out what they were saying, but he watched them disappear down the slope into some caves. He followed them a little distance and found himself in a dark corridor.

The voices were getting louder, as he approached the end of the corridor, and he crouched down and peered into an empty room. There was no sign of Kathleen, and he slowly looked into other areas of the caves. The large cave was where John and his friends were looking at something on the table. It looked like a map. He listened to what they were saying.

"The submarine should be here in twenty-four hours, and Trevor should be on that boat. However, we have enough food and drink to carry us through these hours. Now, where is my sister, Kathleen?" asked John looking at the men. They looked at each other. They had forgotten all about her once they had arranged to meet John. One of them checked, but there was no sign of her.

"She is gone; one of us should have stayed to keep watch," said Alan looking apologetically at John.

"Well, find her. She must be on the island somewhere; the storm has cooled down, and she cannot have gone far," said John in a tone of voice that showed he was not amused.

"I will go," Alan replied.

Colin darted into one of the rooms and watched the tall red-haired man move quickly out of the cave. Colin moved quickly after Alan, and by the time he was on the mound of the abbey, the man had disappeared.

Kathleen stood looking out west and saw the fishing boat. She waved her arm, but obviously Peter had not seen her. She cursed and sat down on a clump of grass. She was cold and began to shiver. Why was she a prisoner on this island, and what was her brother up to? She lay down trying to get out of the wind.

She knew she would be missed, and her brother would have sent someone to look for her. If she was careful, she could look for a boat herself, and attract the attention of Peter, who would come to her rescue. She stood and glanced around her. She was well hidden between the grass and ferns. Her hand was beginning to throb, and she tightened the tissue which was wet with blood. She moved forward toward the abbey keeping to the grassy path, but she kept a look out for any rescue party, which could come up behind her at any moment.

Alan knew the island like the back of his hand, as he always trained and ran each morning before the rest of them were up. He circled near the lighthouse and found some spots of blood on some rocks, so he knew she had come this way and could not be far. He galloped over the grass verges towards the small pier where his boat was hidden, and looking out to sea, he spotted a fishing boat making its way north-east off the island. He only hoped that the woman had escaped in the fishing boat, but he had to make sure that she was still on the island.

Colin found the abbey path hard going and he stopped to get his breath back. He gazed around him, but there was silence, and he began to wonder if Kathleen had managed to get back to Risskay with Peter or perhaps she was still here.

He moved down towards the rocks where Peter had dropped him off. A figure approached from a hill and was coming towards him. He recognised the red-headed guy but could not remember his name.

"Have you seen a woman wandering about?" the guy asked Colin.

"No, I have not seen anyone. Who are you looking for? A woman? Sorry, I have only arrived," replied Colin being very cautious in his reply, as he knew he probably was looking for Kathleen as well. Colin remembered that John had engaged some mercenaries to help him flee the islands, and this was one of them.

Kathleen saw the two figures engaging in conversation down by the shoreline, and she ducked behind some rocks and waited to see what they would do. One was Colin and the red-headed guy that had probably kidnapped her. What was she to do? She could not wait here any longer, as she felt cold, tired and hungry.

Both men parted, and Colin turned and made his way towards the abbey, while the other guy turned and ran up the slope towards the other side.

Kathleen ran down towards Colin and whispered to him. "Colin, oh thank god you are here. I have tried to escape from this dreadful island, but my brother is determined to keep me here."

He did not look at all surprised to see her, and she had this awful thought that he was in this operation her brother had orchestrated. She had no one to turn to now, and Peter was probably away back to the island.

Colin could tell by the expression on her face that she did not believe him, and she started to back away as to escape him. Just then the red-haired guy appeared.

"So that's where you are, trying to escape," he said approaching them.

Kathleen looked at Colin, who was shielding her from the kidnapper, for some sign of what to do next. He felt inside his pocket where he had the small gun. He took the gun and pointed it at the red-haired guy.

"Stay where you are; do not move," warned Colin.

The guy shoved Colin. Colin lost his footing and fell back onto the grass, while Kathleen screamed.

Alan gripped her arm and at the same time told Colin to get up off the ground. His grip was painful, and she struggled to release her arm, but he held her firmly. She glared at him and remarked, "There is no need to be so brutal. You are hurting me."

He took no notice of her, but shoved both of them forward by placing the gun at Colin's back.

She dreaded the very thought of going back into the dingy cave again, as she walked forward past the abbey and down the grassy slope to her brother and the other men.

Chapter Seven

Peter sailed around the island to see if he could spot anyone, but there seemed to be nobody. Where was Colin? As agreed, he decided to get back to the Isle of Risskay as quickly as possible. He drew the boat into the side of the harbour and made his way to the police station, where Bob, the local policeman, would be able to help.

Alastair and Hermione sat in the conservatory. Hermione clipped some shrubs, while Alastair smoked a pipe while watching her. She always seemed so contented. She had always loved gardening and pottering about, while Alastair just liked an easy life by reading the paper and talking to the doctor. They were interrupted by Bob, the policeman, who was banging on the window. Alastair got up and opened the door, which led into the garden.

"What's up, Bob? You don't usually come here, unless you think it is an emergency or a game of golf," said Alastair.

Bob moved into the conservatory and nodded to Hermione. "Well, it's hard to say, but Peter took Colin out to sea and left him on Wisskay. Later, he saw Kathleen and Colin being led away as if by gunpoint. What do you make of that?" asked Bob.

Alastair rubbed his chin and indicated that Bob should come into the house, where it would be easier to speak to him without Hermione getting anxious.

"What is this about gunpoint and Kathleen on the Isle of Wisskay? What the hell is she doing over there? Mind you, I have not seen John or Kathleen for a while, and we were getting worried. What do you make of it?" he asked Bob.

Bob shrugged his shoulders. He took a notebook out and started writing in it. "Now when was the last time you saw Kathleen and John?" asked Bob.

"Now let me see, yes, the other evening at dinner, and we have not seen her since. So that would be two nights ago, and as for John, well, he disappeared with a holdall. He was not here for dinner last night. Kept himself to himself, and we both have hardly seen him," replied Alastair.

"Why do you think she should go to that supposedly haunted island? This is a terrible business; we will have to arrange a rescue mission," said Alastair.

Bob nodded his head in agreement.

"Right! I will inform Peter and Sam, and the doctor of course, in case anyone is hurt badly," said Bob, putting his book away into his pocket. He made his way back to the conservatory, nodding at Hermione as he passed, and got on his bicycle and sped off.

Colin felt the gun in his back, and he held Kathleen's hand, as they made their way down the passage into the caves. The whole place smelt musty and damp, and it was noisy with the sea dashing itself against the rocks.

John looked up as the two of them were herded into

the room. He straightened and smiled at his sister and Colin.

"Welcome to my hideout. I never expected two of you, still the more the merrier." He offered a seat to Kathleen who was glad to sit down.

Colin stood beside her, he clenched his fingers into the palms of his hands, and stared at John. "There was no need to have your sister kidnapped and brought into your sly adventure. She was on a holiday here as always, so what made you think your little scheme is going to work?" said Colin.

John just laughed, and poured out some coffee, placing it in front of Kathleen.

She placed her hands around the mug, feeling the warmth through her hands. She did not say anything; she was too exhausted to comment.

"My dear fellow, you knew I was coming here to do what I had to do, and I'm sorry I brought in Kathleen. I know she is my sister, but arrangements have been made, and afterwards she can continue her holiday with my uncle and aunt. I shall be far away from Scotland to a destination I am not going to mention. Let's sit down and make ourselves comfortable," said John.

The men grabbed a chair and sat around the table waiting to see and hear what John had to say next.

Bob had gathered a group of men from Risskay. The arrangement was that Peter would travel up one side of Wisskay, while Sam did the other side, and a few of them would go onto the island and rescue Colin and Kathleen. Those who possessed guns, knives and other useful instruments would join them. Alastair and the doctor were also to go just in case there was trouble.

Alastair packed a small bag, which contained a revolver and some warm clothes. He was quite excited about the adventure, and it reminded him of his army days. Hermione looked worried, and she asked if everything was going to work out. Alastair assured her that he would get back Kathleen and Colin in one piece. She hated all this fuss and running about, and wondered if she could help in any way. Alastair kissed his wife and set off down towards the hotel where everyone was going to rendezvous. Of course, they would all have a drink or two before setting off.

The submarine, Trevor and additional assistance would be arriving on the Isle of Wisskay at 22.00 hours. The wind had slowly decreased, but the sea was still quite rough. This was good news for John, because as soon as the submarine arrived, the quicker he was off the island. They would hold a party to celebrate before they left. John thought that would make Kathleen happy. The submarine's arrival was a day earlier than planned, and John had some business to sort out before that.

Colin sat beside Kathleen. He knew some of what John was planning, but it would be hard to dissuade John to abandon his whole idea of selling his project.

Kathleen felt tired, and she longed to lie down and sleep, but she kept drinking coffee to keep awake so not to miss anything important. She watched the men discussing over a large map on the table, but they spoke in low voices.

Colin placed his hand on her arm and gave it a tight

squeeze. He whispered, "Peter will have gone back for some help, and your uncle, having been in the army, will arrange a rescue party. Help is coming, but it better come before this submarine comes."

Kathleen looked at him and smiled. "Of course he will save us. I know my uncle – anything for an adventure. He sometimes gets a bit bored on the island, and he goes off to London for company with his old cronies at his club. What they get up to is nobody's business," she said giving a small laugh.

"I could do with some air, and wonder if you will let me go up top. I promise. I will not run away, not this time; anyway, I could not find a boat," she said to John.

John looked up as Kathleen stood up and pointed towards the corridor.

"I feel groggy; I need to have some fresh air," she said to her brother. He came toward her and took her arm. She did look rather peaky. He turned towards the men and waved over Mouska, who came over to them.

"Take my sister out to the abbey for fresh air, but keep an eye on her. See that she does not run away this time," ordered John.

Colin also stood up, but John waved him towards the table and the map.

Kathleen sat on a rock beside the abbey. It was raining a bit, but the wind had died down, and she was so thankful for the fresh air. Mouska stood a little way from her while glancing all around him to see if there were signs of movement. Kathleen gazed out to sea, wondering which way the rescue parties would come. Alastair and Hermione must be sick with worry, especially her aunt. Why had John set up this operation?

Kathleen looked over at Mouska and spoke to him. "Where are you from? I noticed that you are not from the UK?"

He turned around and came up to her. "I am from Turkey, Miss, and I have travelled the world with soldiers fighting different wars, but now I am helping your brother," he remarked staring at her.

"Oh, and what is my brother up to?" she asked smiling at him. At least he may be able to tell her what was going on.

He looked at her, and just then John appeared and shouted at them. "Come on. It is getting dark, cold and wet. Come on, sis, you will catch your death of cold."

"Damn, I might have got an answer from Mouska." She and Mouska walked toward her brother and followed him down into the caves.

John dressed her wound. He poured some whisky on it before placing some dressing and an Elastoplast which was found in the first aid kit. Kathleen screamed as he poured the drink on it.

"Oh, for goodness sake, don't be such a baby girl. How the hell did you do this?" he asked.

"I fell on some rocks and placed my hand to save myself. That is how I cut my hand," she said pulling her hand away from him.

"Right. I think you two should go to another room and rest, as Trevor and company will be here shortly, and we need to tidy up this place." said John.

Colin and Kathleen were ushered down a dark corridor

to another cave slightly bigger than the one she had slept in. Kathleen was annoyed with Colin, as she did not know where she stood with him, as he had obviously known what was happening ever since she came to the island. As soon as she entered the cave, she shivered and turned to Colin.

"Why did you not tell me you were in with my brother and his adventure? Yet, you came all sweet and sugary towards me, knowing damn well you were leading me astray. What are you going to do now? Sail off with his comrades into the glorious sunset? Are you making for China, Russia, the USA, or perhaps, no let me guess, Korea?" said Kathleen, beginning to feel much better since she got this off her chest.

Colin tried to interrupt her, but she was in full flight, and put up her hand so that he could not speak to her.

"Another thing, I noticed that you were not a bit scared when that Alan came up and spoke to you. You knew him all along, and although you pretended you did not know him. Why can't you be honest with me?" she asked as tears began to flow down her cheeks.

Colin stood there facing her, and he knew that she was right. He was not sure of the destination that John was going to, but he did not want to lose her and not now. With the help from her uncle, Peter and the others, he knew that he had to get her off the island somehow.

He pulled her around to face him. Her face was wet with tears, and before she could do anything else, he said, "Look, Kathleen, I promise you that I do not know that red-haired guy called Alan. I knew your brother had men to help him with the submarine. I also know that so-called friend of John's called Trevor, who I do not trust with my life. I met him once in London, as I had just come into the bar; John was saying goodbye to him. He glared at me and walked past me out of the doorway pretty fast.

"I did not dare question your brother who he was or what he wanted. So you see, I do not know everything your brother is up to. Also, I knew he was arranging your kidnap, and all these queer episodes you thought were your imagination. Remember that evening beside the pond? Well, you were almost taken then. I told your brother not to keep frightening you, as I was concerned about your welfare. You've got to believe me."

Kathleen did not know who or what to believe anymore, but she continued standing there looking at him. Was he right and could she trust him, or was she getting all the facts wrong? She was too tired to argue. She drifted into Colin's arms as he hugged her and placed his face into her hair. She put her arms around him; more to keep herself warm than in a loving way.

They sat on a low wooden bench and she laid her head on his shoulder staring into space. She prayed that help would come soon, and she thought of the luxuries of home: a comfortable bed, food and pleasant company. She smiled, and thought if she'd ever get off this island alive, she was going to promise herself never to spend a holiday on an island again.

Colin took the opportunity to kiss her cheek, and Kathleen turned her face towards him. He placed his lips on hers and kissed her hard, hoping that she would return his kiss. She relaxed and kissed him back and placed her arms around his neck. They cuddled close and both fell into a deep sleep.

Chapter Eight

The waves crashed against the rocks, awakening Kathleen. She sat up and looked down at Colin who was still fast asleep. She shivered and wondered if the storm was still battering the coastline. She stepped down from the bench and wandered over to the door which was closed but not locked. Looking down the dark passageway, she could not see or hear anything. How long had she slept? What day was it and where were her brother and his friends?

She moved down the passageway stopping every few minutes to listen, but there was silence. She could see a light in the distance, and she moved quickly towards it. She came to the room where her brother was the last time she had seen him, but it was now empty. She moved towards the exit to the abbey and was hit by a blast of cold air and rain. Quickly retracing her steps, Kathleen rushed back to where she had left Colin. She opened the door and lay down beside him.

Colin put an arm around her, drawing her close to him. "Where have you been? You are soaked," he asked stroking her hair. She wrapped her coat closely to her body. She looked at him and licked her lips.

"I thought I heard movement and went to investigate, but

thank god we are alone. There was nobody there, and they've left us to die in this blasted cave," she said and began to cry.

Colin pulled her closer to him and hugged her. "No, your brother would not do that; he is probably off to meet the submarine and Trevor. I swear that help is coming, and I must get you off this island and back to your uncle somehow." He thought that was where the men had gone, but with the waves hitting the rocks and probably raining as well, it was possible they were sheltering somewhere. He did not want to scare her.

The submarine surfaced on the north of the island, where it could not be seen from the Isle of Risskay. Men stood on the top of the submarine, while two inflatable rubber dinghies were let down to the rough seas, into which they clambered. They made their way to the north-east of the island, where it was more sheltered from the gale-force wind. They carried boxes and made their way towards the abbey and down to the caves.

Most of the boxes contained food and drink, and the men swarmed into the largest cave taking off their wet garments and sitting down.

There were eight men from the submarine including the top man called Trevor Stephens, a six foot tall man with a bald head and piercing greyish blue eyes. He and his men were all dressed in black. He had been born in East London in 1965 and was part of a family of three boys and one girl. He was the eldest. He left school at fifteen and joined the army at seventeen He had fought mainly in the Far East but had also studied to be a captain of a sailing ship. He was very much in charge.

"Well now, here we all are. I think we should celebrate John's adventure, so open the bottles of vodka and have a good time before we set off on our journey."

"Here, I will drink to that, and men, I do appreciate you all for joining me in this adventure. I have thought long and hard about what I am about to do, and I think it is the time in my life to start all over again," said John, raising a glass and drinking. John suddenly remembered about Colin and Kathleen and turned to Trevor.

"Jesus, I forgot about my sister and Colin in the other cave, and I have not seen or heard any sound from that direction. Mouska, go and see if they are still in there. That's a good fellow."

Trevor raised his eyebrows at John and replied, "Your sister is on the island? What does she know about all this? What about the other fellow, Colin? Do I know him? What does he do?" He took a drink from his glass.

John shook his head and said, "She knows nothing of my adventure, and since she was on holiday with me, I felt I had to have her kidnapped. Anyway, she likes a bit of excitement."

"Well, this should be interesting. My men have not seen a woman for quite a long time. You better keep a close eye on her just in case one of them gets any ideas. Anyway, let's look at the map and plan our next move," said Trevor and he made his way over to the table.

Mouska opened the door of the cave and glanced around him. Kathleen and Colin knew they were being summoned by John to make an appearance. Colin held Kathleen's hand and nodded to Mouska. Kathleen clung to Colin's arm, and followed him out the door and down the passageway. Oh, where were they going now? Was her brother letting her escape at last?

The men all stared at Kathleen, as she entered the room. John moved forward and took her arm and sat her down by his side. She felt wretched. Her hair was a mess, and she had no makeup on, as it had all worn off. If she had known that she was going to be a prisoner in these damp caves, she would have at least brought her lipstick. She gazed around her, the men half-smiled, as they stared at her. She felt uncomfortable and looked down at the floor.

Drinks were being poured out from small glasses, and the men paid attention to Trevor, who had taken charge of the proceedings. He glanced at Kathleen and winked at her.

"I am so sorry, my dear, that you find yourself in this predicament, but your brother thought he was doing the best for you. I would frankly have left you to get on with your holiday and not brought you here under these circumstances. As you can see, your brother wants to travel and sell his precious work to any country that will pay him well. We are all here to help," Trevor said as he took his glass and sat down.

All the men clapped and roared at Trevor's speech giving John and Trevor encouragement. Colin glared at Trevor, and Trevor looked at him with a half-smile on his lips. One could tell they disliked each other. Kathleen sipped the drink that was placed in front of her; it was too strong, and she started coughing. If only she had some lemonade to put into the drink.

The pub was noisy with all the men talking at once.

Alastair stood with his drink in his hand and started to issue out orders.

"Now listen here; this is what we are going to do. As soon as the wind dies down and the sea calms, we will set off in two or three boats. I will go with Peter and Bob, and the doctor with Sam and any other person who wants to go with us. Now, as you all know, John, Colin and Kathleen may or may not be on the island. I have a duty to find my niece, as she may have been kidnapped." The men hummed and spoke in low voices.

Alastair continued, "Now we need ropes, lamps, torches, and any handy instruments such as guns, etc. We need all the help we can. We also need someone to stay near a radio in case we need help. So drink up, and let's get organised." He downed his drink and moved over to Peter and Sam.

The winds had calmed down, but the sea was still pretty rough. The crowds of men marched down towards the pier and arranged themselves into the two boats. Some brought out a dinghy and placed a motor onto it. The more boats they had, the more likely the success of the rescue would be. The boats slipped into the foaming sea, as the men pulled their clothing close to their bodies for warmth. Peter took the wheel and made straight for the west side of Wisskay. Meanwhile, Sam made for the east side of the island. Help at last was coming for Kathleen and Colin.

Chapter Nine

The waves swept against the bows of the two fishing boats making their way up the sides of Wisskay. It was still raining but not as heavy as it had been before. The sea still had a slight swell, but the wind had died down, and the men looked ahead raising their binoculars to see if they could see anything moving on the island.

Alastair pointed and said, "Look at the rocks over there, and I can see a small sandy beach. Peter, we should make towards it, and I will go ashore with William. You stay on the boat, and I will signal if I come across Kathleen and Colin. Not too worried about her uncaring brother."

"Right. I will turn starboard and will get as near to land as possible so that you will not get too wet," said Peter. He turned the wheel, and the boat turned slowly making towards the island.

Sam, on the other side of the island, stared ahead and spoke into the mobile phone he had in his hand. He waited for Alastair to reply. The reception was not wonderful, and the connection crackled a lot.

"Hello, Sam. I found a sandy beach this side of the island; where are you exactly?" asked Alastair.

"We are halfway up the island, and are now looking

for a suitable place to land. When we find one, we will go ashore and meet up near the abbey," said Sam.

"Good luck. We will meet at 22:15 at the abbey," said Alastair.

Alastair jumped onto the beach and gave William a hand. William was the younger son of Mr. Mackenzie; the other son was abroad in the army. William was five foot eight inches tall with brown mousey hair, blue eyes and a half grown beard. He was a stocky bloke who did not believe in exercise, and he remained mainly in his bedroom playing computer games. William landed beside Alastair, and he as he looked around, he wondered why he had volunteered for this macho expedition.

Alastair checked his gun and smiled at William.

"Are you going to use that gun if you think we are in danger?" asked William placing his hand in his pockets.

Alastair looked at him, "Do not be afraid, laddie. Stick close to me and only whisper if you want to speak."

They climbed up the banking and moved towards the abbey silhouetted in the darkness; its walls stood out like a ghost. There was silence, and William was scared and frightened, but he did not say anything to Alastair, as they moved forward.

The men were getting drunk, and someone had started to sing. They swayed in their seats in time to the tune the singer was making. Kathleen felt the room grow hot and stuffy, and she began to feel unwell. Her brother and Trevor were enjoying themselves and were joining in the activities. She looked around for Colin and saw him standing near the doorway. He waved at her, and she glanced at her brother before quietly rising from her chair and moving carefully towards the door. She glanced back at her brother and silently moved out of the door. She then ran up towards the entrance of the caves and into the fresh air. She stood and breathed in the damp cold air. What route could she take to get off this island and home to her aunt and uncle?

Colin had followed her and stood beside her taking her arm, "Are you okay, you look rather peaky."

Kathleen turned towards him. "I feel hellish, and I want to go home. I do not care about my brother and his merry men, and I don't care if I never see him again. How could he do this to me on my annual holiday? It is not fair," she said bursting into tears. Colin placed an arm around her and hugged her.

They heard a movement, and Colin signalled for Kathleen to keep quiet. He moved towards the abbey, took his gun out and moved slowly.

Kathleen was alone until a tall figure came towards her. It was one of the sailors, who had obviously been relieving himself nearby.

"Hello, little lady. How about a little kiss and cuddle, eh?" he said with slurred speech moving towards her.

Kathleen moved backwards, as he approached her. She put out her hands to stop him, and the next thing she remembered was falling backwards landing on a grassy mound. She tried to sit up but felt a weight across her legs. She tried to scream, as she noticed that the sailor had a knife sticking out of his back. He was obviously dead and lying across her legs. God, what next? She had to get up and move away before anything else happened. She managed to untangle her legs from the body, and she knelt and looked around in the gloom. Where was Colin, and who had killed the sailor?

She got her bearings as she saw the outline of the abbey, and she moved to the right of it, slowly crawling to where the sea was bashing against the rocks. If she made her way towards the lighthouse again, she may be able to spot a boat, or even a fishing boat. Perhaps Peter was out looking for her. The going was tough, and she crawled along the edge like a crab while the sea continued to thunder below. She had travelled some distance but not enough to get to the lighthouse.

William and Alastair stood on the north side of the abbey, where they were greeted by Sam, the doctor and the policeman.

"Good we are all here, but perhaps we had better split up. William and I will stay on the west side while you two travel the east side. We do not want to attract attention just in case there is an army of folk here," said Alastair. They checked their weapons. All of them had guns except for poor William who did not have anything to defend himself.

Colin found the body of the sailor and dragged him into the bushes nearby. He pulled the knife out of the body wiping the blood on the grass. Where had Kathleen disappeared to? Had she gone back to the caves and her brother, or had she tried to escape? He moved towards the abbey and came upon Alastair and a terrified William. He was glad they had successfully arrived on the island.

"What is happening? Where are Kathleen and John?" asked Alastair.

"Her brother has some men in the caves below and will be leaving soon to board a submarine berthed north of the island. John is aiming to sell his secret scientific G85 project to any country that will buy it, and he is leaving the UK for good. Kathleen knows that he will be leaving the island, but he is very secretive about where he is going," said Colin.

Alastair rubbed his chin and stared at Colin. "So this is what it is all about – espionage; and where does my niece fit into this adventure? Where is she, by the way?" asked Alastair.

"I was with her, as she was not feeling too good; she had come up to get some fresh air. One of the sailors approached her, and she must have tripped and fell backwards. I am afraid I killed him with a knife, as I did not want John and company to hear any rumpus up here. She has disappeared, and I have also been looking for her. You must get her off the island," said Colin.

"Spread out and look for her! Once we have found her, get her back to one of the boats and back to Risskay. That goes for you too, Colin; you should not be mixed up with this so-called nonsense that John has thought up, but it's too late now. Blasted fellow! He's potentially causing volunteers to get hurt."

They spread out and started looking for Kathleen.

Kathleen was exhausted; she lay down between the high ferns and hoped she would be found sooner rather than later. Where had Colin disappeared to? He must have heard the sailor talk to her. It was a good job someone had killed the sailor, as she hated the idea of being raped. She heard voices and raised her head to see if she could see anyone. She got up and moved down the west side towards the abbey. She wondered if John had missed her yet.

William had split up from Alastair, and he moved north through the vegetation, sometimes falling through the ferns, which were high enough to hide anyone from the outside world. He was dreaming as usual thinking of the latest song he had heard on the radio and did not see the person approaching him.

Kathleen could hear someone coming towards her, and she stood still, as there was nowhere really to hide. She waited for the figure as it came closer, and she could make out it was someone but not who it was. The figure suddenly stopped realising that there was someone else on the path.

"Who are you? Please tell me who you are!" said Kathleen speaking quietly, hoping it was not one of the sailors.

William stood still and realised that it was the woman. He spoke to her. "My name is William, and I have come to fetch you. Your uncle is also here to rescue you."

Kathleen burst into tears, and she hugged William clinging onto his arms. She was so relieved that someone had finally come! William was taken aback at her reaction and stood like a dummy with his arms by his side. They moved slowly down the worn grassy path; Kathleen clinging for dear life onto poor William.

When Alistair came into view, Kathleen immediately ran to her uncle and hugged him; she was so glad to see him.

"Hush, my lass, everything is going to be alright. You

are wet through and through and cold. I will take you to Peter's boat where you can rest."

Colin suddenly appeared, and he was relieved to see her safe. She looked at him and burst into tears. She left her uncle and moved to where Colin was standing. His hair and clothes were also soaked, but he smiled as he placed his arm around her.

They moved towards the sandy shore, and Kathleen was hauled up onto Peter's boat. He was glad to see her and immediately took her to a small room where a small put-me-up bed had been placed. Hot drinks were given all round. Colin was glad of the warm drink, and due to Alistair's thoughtfulness, he managed to change his clothes and dry his hair with a towel. He was going back to John. He wanted to stop him getting on that submarine, and he needed all the help he could get.

Chapter Ten

Kathleen suddenly felt exhausted, and she quickly changed into warmer clothes and stretched out on the bed. She felt better after the sweet hot coffee.

Peter looked in at her and smiled. He said, "You must be really very tired after these events. Now that you are looking brighter, I am going to see what Alastair and Colin are doing. They were going back to stop your brother from boarding that submarine."

Kathleen was horrified and said, "Oh, my god, no. You will all be killed; let's just go back to Auntie Hermione. She must be terrified and worried."

Just then Colin appeared. "Hey, you are looking better already," Colin smiled at her.

She gazed at him and thought he had just saved her life, so why does he now want to help my brother. "I hear you and Uncle Alastair want to return to the island to stop my brother from boarding the submarine. Please do not go! You will all be killed, and what will happen to me then?" she pleaded looking at him.

He knew she was upset at her brother's behaviour and the stupidity of him wanting to go to far-away places. He sat down on the bed, and closed the curtain making the room private. He leant over and kissed her lips, and she put her arms around his neck drawing him down to her. She did not want him to leave her, and she looked up at him and said, "You know, I think I have fallen in love with you, but you don't look surprised."

Colin smiled and gave a little laugh.

"I fell in love with you the moment I saw you in London. I persuaded your brother to let me come on this holiday; I wanted to see you again, and I am not disappointed." He placed his hand on her breast, and slipped his hand under her jumper so that he could touch it. He bent his head down and kissed her nipple. She smiled at him, touching his hair and running her hand over his face. She knew what he was going to do next and half-smiled to herself.

Colin undid her jeans and pulled them down; he unzipped his trousers and placed himself on top of her. He was not sure whether she was a virgin, but he would find out. He waited to see if she would protest, but she just sprawled back, closed her eyes and joined in the movements.

She still had her arm around him after they had both enjoyed their sexual pleasures. He tossed his hair back from his face and smiled at her.

"Be safe and wait for me. I will do my very best to try and talk to your brother and get him to stop what he is hoping to achieve and do," he said.

"Please be very careful and watch your back with that Trevor. He sounds charming but can be dangerous," she pleaded, sitting up.

Colin joined Alastair and Peter who were standing at the stern of the boat; they knew that Kathleen and Colin wanted to say goodbye. Alastair smiled at Colin, as he guessed what both of them had been up to.

"Peter will stay here and guard the boat, and when I let off a flare, it'll be the signal for you to start the boat and approach the north of the island to stop the submarine leaving. I have spoken to Sam and company, and they will do exactly the same on the east side of the island. Keep Kathleen sedated with these pills, as we do not want a woman running about as she could get hurt. Is that all clear?" Alastair asked looking at Peter.

Peter nodded his head, and they moved to the starboard side of the vessel. Colin and Alastair went ashore and made their way towards the centre of the abbey. They checked their guns, but this time William stayed on board Peter's boat just in case Peter needed any help.

"We need to make our way to the caves near the abbey. That is where we will find John and company. It is getting late, so they are bound to come up and make their way to the north for the submarine," said Colin.

"Right, my boy, lead on. If I remember rightly, there is another entrance quite near here, but it is a very long time since I was on this island. Follow me and keep quiet. Speak only in a whisper. We should come up near the large cave, and I bet they are all in that cave. Am I right?" asked Alastair.

They slipped down an embankment which led into a dark passageway. They both had torches and the passageway stretched for a couple of hundred feet. There were spiders on the ceiling and walls, and they were glad that Kathleen was not with them. It was very dusty, and it spread onto their clothes, as they moved slowly along.

They heard voices in the distance. Colin and Alastair both stood still, listening. "They were having a farewell party when I left with Kathleen. All of them were either drunk or pretending to be, as they were in full voice," remarked Colin.

They eventually came out of the passageway into a dark corridor, and they held their torches facing their feet, just in case anybody was near. Both of them held their guns as they walked quietly down the corridor. They came beside the cave where Colin and Kathleen had stayed before the arrival of John, Trevor and the sailors. They both did not want to return the same way as they had come, so they made their way towards the large cave where the men were packing up and getting ready to leave.

John and Trevor started packing up; they wanted to leave the island before daylight. John looked around him and noticed that Kathleen and Colin were not in the cave.

"Where are Kathleen and Colin? They do not seem to be here. Have you seen them?" John asked looking at Trevor.

Trevor looked around him. He had drunk too much vodka, and he was already getting a headache. "No, I cannot say I have noticed; we were all having a good time."

The men were moving at the back of the cave, and three of them came towards John. "The woman and the man went out to get some fresh air, as the woman looked ill," said the bearded sailor.

John looked up from the map he had on the table. "I want volunteers to go and look for them, and bring them back here," he ordered. What a nuisance his sister was! He should have just left her at his uncle's.

The men nodded, and Alan also went with them, as he knew the island better than most of them. Alan had other ideas; he was fed up being cooped up on the island. He had to find one of the boats and make his way back to civilisation. He let the men run on, and looking to the east, he noticed a light shining. Was there a boat out there? He climbed the embankment and slipped on some rocks, while he held his hand to shield his eyes. There was definitely something out there with a light. The fishermen were surely not out fishing at this time of night. Alan turned back and started to run up towards the lighthouse. That was where she had gone before. Should he let her escape? Where was the bright boy, Colin? Where had he disappeared to?

Dr. MacNicol lit a cigarette and gazed around him, as he stood under one of the ruined arches of the abbey. What was happening? The silence was killing him. Sam stood a little way from him with a torch in his hand. They had landed from the boat and had left two men on board. They wondered where Alastair and Colin were. They were supposed to meet once again beside the abbey.

Frank, the Irishman, and Mouska started to carry large boxes out of the cave, as most of the men had been sent out to search for Colin and Kathleen. Frank stopped, lifted a silver flask of brandy and took a long sip. He turned to Mouska and whispered, "God, I am thirsty, and I am now longing to get off this damn island. I do not know what Trevor and John are playing at, but hopefully we will not be going on that submarine."

Mouska nodded his head and said, "Perhaps the

woman has left the island and is back home. We are wasting our time here, and by the way, when are we going to get paid?

Frank lit a cigarette, let the smoke fill his lungs and thought for a moment. He picked up the boxes and marched up the middle of the abbey towards the rocks near the submarine. Mouska followed him.

Sam had noticed the two men carrying something quite heavy, and he walked over to the doctor and said, "There are two of them lifting a heavy item. Perhaps we should follow them, and see where they are going."

The doctor put out his cigarette and whispered, "We were supposed to meet Alastair and Colin, but we have not seen or heard from them for some time. Maybe it would be a good idea to follow these guys and see where they go."

Sam nodded, and Dr. MacNicol moved down through the worn path following the dim light the two men were showing, as they moved ahead.

Colin slipped passed the cave where Trevor and John were leaving. Alastair was near the small room with the bed, table and chair. They decided that Alastair was to stay in hiding until Colin returned, and they hoped that Colin would be united with the doctor and Sam, who were waiting for them near the abbey.

Alan reached the lighthouse in no time and saw the outline of the submarine. There was no sign of Kathleen or Colin, so he made his way back through the bracken, stopping now and again to see if he could hear or see any movement. He stopped suddenly and crouched low while two sailors approached talking in low voices; as they passed him, he stood up and lifted the knife he had in his hand. With two strokes, he slit their throats and let their bodies fall onto the bracken. He now made his way towards the abbey.

Chapter Eleven

Colin made his way to the middle of the abbey, where he hoped to meet Sam and the doctor, but there was nobody there. Where had they disappeared to? He shrugged his shoulders and stood for a minute looking around him. He heard someone coming, and he dropped to the ground and waited. Four men appeared talking in low voices, and they passed Colin making their way back to the caves.

Colin stood up and walked towards the north of the island. He stumbled across two dead bodies lying in the bushes, and as he looked more closely, he noticed that their throats had been cut. They certainly would not have known what had happened to them. Who had done this sort of thing? They were just sailors from the submarine. He started to run, and as he came towards the north-east part of the island, he saw a figure near a boat who was trying to escape. He silently moved forward to have a better look.

Alan had managed to get to one of the motor boats, but it would not start. He was pulling the starter rope in the hope that the engine would fire up. He did not hear Colin approach. Colin slipped down the small sandy path holding his gun towards the figure at the boat. He wasted no time and spun the boat around, knocking Alan into the water.

"What the bloody hell," shouted Alan, fumbling for his knife.

"You bastard, where were you going? Did you kill those poor sailors in the bushes?" yelled Colin, hitting Alan and sending him backwards into the cold but shallow water.

Alan was taken by surprise and he stood up. He hit out at Colin, but Colin ducked. The two of them hit each other, falling into the water, until a shot rang out. Both men sought cover and slipped onto the banking. Someone must have heard the motor and come to investigate. Colin moved further up the grassy slope but kept his head well down. Colin knew he had to be very careful. Now, he did not trust Alan or any other man associated with John.

The doctor and Sam heard the gunshot. They were on the north of the island facing the large submarine whose ghostly shape lay in the bay. They looked at each other and crept behind some bushes. "Did you hear a gunshot or was it my imagination?" asked the doctor looking at Sam.

"Yes, I heard it too. I think we should make our way back to the abbey to meet Alastair and Colin. This is getting dangerous if they are using weapons."

They moved off, as they had lost sight of the two men who were carrying boxes.

Frank and Mouska also heard the gunshot, as they were placing the boxes beside a dinghy hidden by some bushes. They looked at each other and knew at once that they had company besides the sailors and John. They wondered where Alan was. He had been sent off to find the woman.

Kathleen woke from a deep sleep and wondered where she was. She pulled back the blanket and swung her legs off the small bed. She tidied herself up and went outside onto the deck. The whole boat smelled of fish. She found William and Peter looking through binoculars towards the abbey.

Peter turned around and smiled at her. "Feeling better now? I think there must be some action on now. We just heard a gunshot," said Peter.

"I think that's what woke me up. Oh, I hope Colin and John are okay," she said leaning on a rail.

"Would you like some tea or coffee to freshen you up?" asked Peter.

"Yes, I will go and put on the kettle, while you keep watch," she said as she made her way back inside the cabin.

Alastair was fed up waiting for Colin, and he took the opportunity, after making sure that the coast was clear, to make his way up to the abbey. He found Colin walking towards him.

"Where have you been? I have been hiding in that cold cave for ages! John and company are beginning to pack up, so it will not be long before they move off to the submarine," stated Alastair, rubbing his hands together.

"I ran into a spot of bother. Alan was trying to get off the island, and I tried to stop him. Someone fired a shot and I came back here, but god knows where Alan went. He is a dangerous fellow, and I think he may have killed two sailors," Colin said.

"What we should do is to fire off some flares, so that both boats know to move towards the north of the island but not too close," said Alastair.

"Perhaps wait until the procession of men from the caves start moving towards the submarine," Colin said.

They agreed, and at that moment, the doctor and Sam appeared.

"Where have you been?" Alastair asked looking at them.

"We followed two men who were carrying boxes towards the north. We then heard a gunshot, so we turned back," the doctor replied.

"Well, I think it is time to let off the flares, so the boats can make their way towards the submarine," said Alastair taking them out of a rucksack he had been carrying.

Just then they heard voices and they ducked behind a wall of the abbey. They peered out to see who was coming. Six men appeared making their way up the steep embankment from the caves below towards the submarine. Alastair signalled to Sam and the doctor to return to their boat in readiness to move up towards the north of the island.

Hermione and Charlie, the dog, stood on the pier on the Isle of Risskay. The other people gathered there gazed into the darkness, but all they could see was a small light in the distance. The villagers stood beside her talking in low voices, wondering what was happening. They thought they heard gunfire but were not sure.

"Can you see anything out there, Scott?" a man asked who was standing near the sea wall.

"Na, I canna see a damn thing. It's too dark, and anyway, that island is too far away to see anything," he replied.

"It must be near on four o'clock, and it will be getting light soon," said Hermione turning and talking to the man beside her.

"Aye, and soon Alastair and company will return with your niece, Kathleen, that is if she is on the island," said the man. Hermione nodded and wrapped her coat around her body, as there was a keen wind blowing.

They stood in silence waiting to see what would happen next.

Kathleen nearly jumped out of her skin when the flares went up. She knew that this was the start of the blockage of any escape route for her brother, Trevor and their companions.

Peter started up the engine of his boat and moved forward towards the north west of the island.

Sam and the doctor, who had returned to their boat, did the same thing, but moving north-east of the island. The smaller boats lying in the south of the island started up. One followed Sam and the other, Peter.

Chapter Twelve

John and Trevor were surprised to find some of the guards back so soon. John shouted over to them, "Where have you been and where is my sister?"

They shook their heads, and a voice spoke from behind the guards.

"Your sister is in a very safe place. If you were thinking of taking her with you, I know full well she does not want to leave her uncle and aunt," said Colin, appearing in the doorway. He had silently moved down towards the caves behind the sailors.

John stared at Colin. He had guessed that Colin had found her and got her safely ashore.

"Well, is she back at Risskay, or is she still on this island?" John asked.

Colin smiled and replied, "I am not at liberty to say. Think, man, of what she has been through these few days! She is scared stiff and is wondering what is going to happen to her brother. Are you at all worried my friend, or are you more interested in getting somewhere in the world to sell your precious experiment?" asked Colin.

The men moved forward towards Colin, but Colin stood still. He had his gun in his pocket. He did not want to hurt anyone else, but if necessary, he would use it.

John and Trevor picked up their belongings, and John looked at his watch with difficulty. Colin was blocking their exit. John looked at Trevor, and they both walked towards the doorway.

Unknown to Colin, someone had crept into the caves and hit him over the head with their gun. Colin fell to the ground, and John and Trevor stepped over him.

Frank placed his gun into his pocket, and nodded to John to say that he had taken care of Colin. He followed the men up to the abbey and on to where the submarine was waiting.

Alan crawled forward towards the abbey. He wondered if there were more men on the island ready to help Colin after the flares went up. Certainly, he saw the lights from fishing boats both side of the abbey, and they looked as though they were travelling northwards. He wondered where Mouska and Frank had disappeared to. He had not seen them for a while.

Alan lifted his gun and waited to see who would come up first from the caves, as he knew he had not seen John or Trevor or any other sailors.

The doctor and Bob, the policeman, stepped into the smaller boat and left Sam and others on board to keep a look-out. They thought it would be best to give Alastair and Colin a helping hand in case there was trouble.

Alastair wondered where Colin was as he stood in the shadows of the abbey. A figure approached the abbey, but it moved away from Alastair and disappeared towards the caves. Just then, John and Trevor and a few sailors appeared and moved quickly as if someone was in pursuit. It was getting light now and that made it more difficult to hide.

It was tough going through the undergrowth and John stopped several times to get his breath back. He was not as fit as Trevor or Alan, who always exercised in the morning. The launch was parked north-west of the island.

Alastair had seen John and company moving off, and he continued to wonder where Colin was. He moved slowly down the slopes to the caves and took his gun out in preparation for an attack. He found Colin rubbing his head, and trying to sit up.

"What happened to you? Did you manage to stop John?" Alastair asked as he pulled Colin up to his feet.

"No, someone hit me over the head, and I cannot remember anything else. Have John and company managed to get to the submarine?" asked Colin. Colin and Alastair moved out of the caves and on the grassy verge of the abbey. The doctor and Bob appeared and approached them.

"Where have you two been? We have seen John moving north, so we had better stop them quick before that submarine leaves," said the doctor.

"Ready, now let's split up; two going north-east and the others north-west," said Alastair, who always wanted to be in charge.

Alan crouched behind a grassy mound watching the small group of men. He also wanted to stop John. He had not been paid for several weeks, and he wanted out. He could not care less if John got away to wherever he was going. He pulled out his knife and started to move quickly to the north of the island. He travelled fast through the undergrowth, jumping over bushes and ferns.

Alastair fired a shot into the air and followed Colin into the undergrowth, while the doctor and the policeman made their way to the other side of the abbey.

Alastair laughed a little while running his hand over his moustache. "That will stop them in their tracks. It will also give me a chance to get nearer to them to stop them."

"Where is Alan? Have you seen or heard him?" asked Colin, turning his head to Alastair.

"No, cannot say I have seen him; god, I forgot about him," said Alastair. The two men stood still listening, and they heard shouts away in the distance.

The doctor and Bob also stopped and listened. Suddenly a shot was heard and the two of them ducked down by the ferns. Someone was firing a gun, but their instinct knew it was not Alastair who'd fired it.

Alan stopped in his tracks. He could see John, Trevor and some of the sailors standing and listening. There was another shot, and John and Trevor lay flat on the ground, not daring to move.

"Jesus, who the hell is firing at us?" asked John.

He looked at Trevor who smiled and said, "We forgot Alan. He was trying to escape earlier on, and one of the men fired at two other men who were fighting by one of the boats. He is probably fed up, as he never got paid."

"I never trusted that Alan bloke, so perhaps it is he who is shooting at us," said John.

The two men and sailors lay low trying to work out how

they were going to approach the submarine without getting shot.

Frank and Mouska were ahead of John and Trevor. They moved fast towards the launch after they heard the gunfire. They wanted to get off the island, and as they untied the rope holding the launch, they jumped into it at the same time.

Alan raised his gun and fired in the direction of John and Trevor. He heard a sailor scream in pain. There was a moment's silence before another gunshot was heard. Alan raised his head to see who he had hit, but another shot rang out, and he felt a pain in his own shoulder. He was hit. He rolled over in the heather, slipped off his coat, and ripped part of his shirt so that he could stop the bleeding now running down his arm. He cursed and drew out his knife. He fell forward still looking at where he thought John and Trevor were situated. He crawled through the shrubbery towards them, but as he knelt to throw the knife, he fell forward onto his face, as a knife was stuck in his back.

Colin and Alastair moved forward quietly, as they had witnessed the shooting between John and somebody else. Colin came across the body of Alan. He felt for a pulse but shook his head. As Alan was now dead, where were the other sailors and John?

Bob and the doctor decided to return to the fishing boat and make haste towards the submarine before it left. They got into their small boat and rowed towards Sam's boat. They could not use the engine due to the noise it would make. They boarded the fishing boat and hoped that Alastair and Colin were safe.

John and Trevor made a dash for the launch, as the bullets flew over their heads. One of the sailors fell backwards into the water, as a bullet hit his forehead. John and Trevor jumped into the launch just as it was taking off. This was the second boat, as Frank and Mouska were now at the submarine. They were climbing up the sides and hoping that they were now not the target of the bullets.

Colin aimed at the two figures running towards the rocks and water, but he missed them. There were three sailors now in the water making a great attempt to get to the submarine. Colin caught his foot on a boulder and fell down towards some rocks. He badly hit his right arm and he heard the crack of his bone; he knew that he had broken his arm.

Alastair searched for Colin who had vanished. He crouched in the ferns whispering Colin's name. Surely he was not shot or wounded! He could hear motors in the distance, and he knew that John had escaped.

Chapter Thirteen

The small boats circled around Peter's, and Johnnie, a local fisherman, signalled that he wanted Kathleen to come with him, so that he could take her back to the Isle of Risskay. The gunfire had unnerved him, and he wanted her safely back home.

Peter took Kathleen's arm and threw down a rope ladder, so that she could step into the other boat. She gingerly did what she was told and took her time in descending the ladder.

Peter shouted down, "Take good care of her. I will soon be returning hopefully with her brother, Colin and Alastair." He waved them off before immediately turning his attention to moving closer to the submarine.

Sam stood in the wheelhouse of the boat. He turned it so that it would block the submarine. They noticed that John and Trevor and a few remaining sailors were boarding the submarine. The engines had started and water was beginning to flow over the decks. The sailors and Trevor were moving down a hatch on the deck followed by John.

Trevor was in front of John, but he suddenly turned and punched John hard on the shoulder with all his strength.

John was taken by surprise and fell onto the swirling decks of the submarine.

"You will not be needed anymore. I have what I wanted, so goodbye, my friend!" shouted Trevor, laughing hysterically before dropping into the well of the submarine.

John lay on the decks trying to get his breath back, and he shouted out, "Help me! Someone, for god's sake do not leave me to die." He was washed off the submarine and into the water.

Peter looked on in horror as the submarine dived between the fishing boats. There was no sign of John, and one or two of the smaller boats moved forward to search the water. He was so glad Kathleen had not witnessed her brother's drowning.

Alastair stood on the north of the island watching what had happened. Where was Colin? He had to find him and get some help.

Colin kept falling in and out of consciousness, and his arm hurt like hell. He groaned and tried to yell out, but every time he moved, unbearable pain shot up his arm and shoulder.

Alastair heard a soft moan. He found Colin lying by some rocks, and he looked like he was badly wounded. "God almighty! Man, what has happened to you? Did someone shoot at you? Well, the submarine has gone, and I am afraid to say that John was knocked off the submarine by his good friend Trevor. The men are out looking for him. I will get in touch with the RAF rescue, and you will be uplifted to hospital, probably Oban," said Alastair planting himself down beside Colin.

Colin looked at Alastair and said: "What happened to Kathleen? Did she get off this damn island to safety? God, I hope so." He closed his eyes, and once again drifted into unconsciousness.

Alastair moved away to use his phone to call the emergency services and the doctor for more immediate help. Colin remained in the same position when he awoke but was afraid to move. He hoped that the doctor could give him some painkillers.

Doctor MacNicol, after getting his medical bag off the boat, knelt down. Colin opened his eyes and was thankful to see the doctor. He took out a syringe and needle, drew up some pain medication and injected Colin.

"That will kill the pain until the helicopter turns up. You have been in the wars, my friend," said the doctor.

"I heard that Kathleen was taken back to Risskay before the dreadful scene with her poor brother drowning," said the doctor, placing a cushion of sorts under Colin's head.

It was dawn when the helicopter landed on the Isle of Wisskay. The boats had spent hours circling the area where the submarine had submerged, but there was no sign of John.

Bob, the policeman, stayed on the island with Sam and the doctor, as the authorities were informed. They now expected an inspector from Glasgow to come and take statements.

Colin was transferred onto a stretcher with his arm strapped to a splint made from a piece of wood. He was uplifted, placed into the helicopter and taken off to the hospital in Oban.

The bodies of the dead sailors and Alan were laid out in the middle of the abbey. They were covered in sheeting to hide their injuries.

Bob and the doctor were tired and worn out, as they had not had any sleep over the past twelve hours. They were also very hungry. Alastair managed to phone back to the island of Risskay and asked for some sandwiches and coffee or tea be brought out to the men left on the island.

Bob was preparing some background notes for the Inspector when he arrived, so that all the facts would be correctly given. Alastair went back home with the medicine to give to Kathleen, to have some breakfast and a rest.

Chapter Fourteen

With the medicine, Kathleen slept for nearly twenty-four hours. She felt revived after her long rest. Alastair told her that Colin had broken his arm and been taken to the hospital in Oban.

The next day Inspector Formby arrived from Glasgow constabulary and started asking questions regarding her brother's presumed death and the murder of the sailors. He also examined the caves on Wisskay and the surrounding area.

The inspector was a thin man with grey hair and a beard. He stood with his raincoat hanging off his shoulders as he took notes. He questioned Sam, Peter, the doctor and Alastair. He left Kathleen until last, since she had broken down after hearing her brother's tragic news. He informed Interpol to see if they could stop the submarine, but they informed him that this would be difficult as nobody knew the intended destination.

Kathleen took another ten days off work due to the circumstances, and the funeral would have to wait until a body was found. Kathleen became very withdrawn, kept to her room and only turned up at meal times. Alastair and Hermione were worried, and they encouraged her to be outdoors rather than moping in her room. They knew she cried a lot, and to make her happy, it was suggested that Alastair and Kathleen go to Oban and visit Colin in hospital.

Inspector Formby had questioned Kathleen regarding her relationship with her brother. He asked why her brother wanted her kidnapped in the first place. After all, John could have easily have left her with her aunt and uncle to enjoy her holiday. Kathleen did not know why she had been kidnapped and kept prisoner in the caves. It was only Colin and her uncle who had managed to get her off the island and somewhere safe.

Inspector Formby left the island of Risskay to write up a report. He said he would be in touch if he had any information regarding the submarine. Also he was going to look into the background of Frank, Mouska, and Trevor. He hoped that they would find John's body. The bodies of Alan and the sailors were taken to the morgue in Glasgow.

Kathleen bought flowers and some grapes and made her way to the hospital to Ward 12. She was nervous about meeting Colin again, and she clung on to Alastair's arm for support. She looked pale, and although she had coloured her cheeks with rouge so that she did not look like a ghost, she still felt awful. She took several breaths before entering the ward, and she pushed Alastair in front of her.

Colin was sitting up in bed, resting on pillows, as he had been waiting three days already for an x-ray and he was looking forward to getting his arm into plaster. He had grown a beard which made him very attractive. Kathleen smiled but let Alastair go forward to greet Colin.

"How are you, my boy? You look well, and the arm I can see is getting better," said Alastair shaking Colin's other hand.

Colin smiled and looked over at Kathleen. He said to Alastair, "Have they found John yet?"

Alastair placed a finger over his lips, shook his head, and stepped aside so that Kathleen could come forward.

Kathleen smiled again at Colin and bent down to kiss him on the cheek. She wanted to cry, but she fought back the tears that were forming in her eyes. He brought his face up so that he could kiss her on the lips. It was a soft kiss, and she suddenly burst into tears and sat on the chair beside the bed. Colin looked at Alastair, who tiptoed out of the room so that they could be alone.

"Do not cry, my love. I will be out soon, and all will turn out alright. You have been through a drama with your brother and his friends who were no friends at all," he said stroking her hand.

She tried to smile and looked at him and said, "My brother is dead. After working all those years on his project, he was murdered for greed and money. How could he do this to me? Did you know where he was actually going? If you do know, tell the Inspector so he can catch those bastards, especially Trevor. God, he was charming and yet cool and dangerous; even I recognised that."

Colin smiled and squeezed her hand. He loved her and did not want to lose her. He knew that after he left hospital he had to find another job. He could not face returning to Southampton to work. "My dear sweet Kathleen, I do love you so much, and I want to take you on a long holiday somewhere of your choice. My answer to your question regarding your brother's destination is this, and it is only a guess. I think he was heading for China," said Colin taking a drink of water.

There was silence in the room, and Kathleen felt her heart miss a beat. China, why China? She shook her head in disbelief. She got off her seat and wandered over to the window before turning back and looking at Colin. "I cannot believe that he was destined to go to China. Why did he not tell me? I am going to tell that inspector that is where the submarine was going, but what part of China? Do you know?"

Colin took another sip of water, as he felt his throat become dry. He looked at her and replied, "No, I don't know which part, but please tell that inspector to have the Chinese authorities watch all of the ports. Now come here and give me a hug and a kiss." He held his arm towards her.

Kathleen sat on the edge of the bed and buried her face in his chest. She did not want to lose Colin. He been so good in rescuing her from her brother and Trevor, but she could not stop wondering why she was kidnapped. Was he going to take her with him? She looked up at Colin and said, "Where are you going when you leave here? Are you going back to Southampton even after all that has happened?"

Colin looked past her at Alastair who had come back into the room. Alastair had two coffees in his hand and had heard what Kathleen had said to Colin.

"I will not be going back to Southampton, as questions will be asked about John. To be honest, I do not want to be involved in a whole lot of questions. I will hand in my notice after I have found a suitable post."

Alastair passed the hot coffee to Kathleen and said, "Here, my dear, drink this; it will do you good. We will leave poor Colin to rest now."

Kathleen took the paper cup and drank out of it. She handed the cup back to Alastair before bending down and kissing Colin's lips. She said, "I love you, and I will come back to see you tomorrow."

Colin held her hand and squeezed it. He whispered, "I look forward to seeing you tomorrow; I will let you know when I can leave the hospital."

Alastair took Kathleen's arm and they left the room with Kathleen gazing back at Colin sitting up in bed.

Alastair and Kathleen stayed in the Alexandria Hotel on Oban's seafront. Kathleen had a good view of the bay, and she sat watching the activity of boats and people rushing by. She still did not have an appetite and played with her food at meal times.

Alastair insisted she took a walk with him along the promenade to get some fresh air, and they took a trip over to Iona, but the weather was too windy and the sea too rough to venture over to Staffa, the location of Fingal's Cave.

The next day Kathleen went alone to visit Colin in hospital, and found him sitting in the general lounge with other patients. He was talking to a blonde lady sitting opposite him, and both of them were laughing at some joke. Kathleen stood watching them, and she felt a pang of jealousy. She moved forward and said in a quiet voice,

"Hello, Colin. How are you today?" She glanced at the woman, who smiled back at her.

The woman said, "Your man and his jokes are hilarious; anyway, I will leave you now." And with that she guided her wheelchair and moved off to the other side of the room.

Kathleen pulled up a chair and sat opposite Colin.

"Who was that lady? You seemed to be enjoying each other's company," said Kathleen.

"Aren't you going to kiss me and say hello?" asked Colin, who noticed that Kathleen appeared to be a wee bit jealous of him speaking to the other woman.

"Of course, I am," replied Kathleen, leaning over to give him a peck on the cheek. Colin held her arms and planted a kiss on her lips. Kathleen pulled back in embarrassment. She wasn't comfortable with public displays of affection.

"What have you been up to since yesterday? Where is Alastair?" asked Colin leaning back in his chair while looking at her. She still looked pale and withdrawn.

"We went by boat to Iona, but it was too rough to visit Staffa, where the famous Fingal's Cave is. Both of us enjoyed the outing; I know that my uncle was trying his best to cheer me up."

"That sounds great. I have never been there but may try and visit it one day. Please give me your home telephone number; I will be leaving in a day or two, and we should keep in touch," said Colin.

Kathleen pulled out a piece of paper and pen from her jacket pocket, scribbled her phone number on it and passed it to Colin.

"I am going back to London next week. I want to leave

that island and the memories. How about you?" she said looking at him.

"I will be discharged pretty soon, and then I must look for some work. But don't worry, when I am down in London, I will be in touch," said Colin.

Kathleen got up to leave, and as she turned to him to say goodbye she noticed the other woman returning.

Kathleen and Alastair returned to the Isle of Risskay for a few more days before packing for her return journey to London and work. There was still no sign of John's body, so the funeral, if there was ever going to be one, would be delayed. Kathleen felt she could not face returning to the island in the future but was sad to leave her kind uncle and aunt.

She did not go back to Oban to visit Colin, and she was not sure if he would ever get in touch with her, after what happened at the infirmary. When she arrived in Oban after her sea journey, she did not know if Colin had left the hospital, but she boarded the train to Glasgow, where she would catch the sleeper to London Euston.

Chapter Fifteen

Kathleen worked in Holborn, the centre of London, and she settled back into her secretarial job and was glad that other employees did not ask about her holiday. Of course, they had heard rumours that she had been kidnapped, but they did not enquire what the outcome was.

Her boss, Mr. John Archer, asked if everything was alright. Kathleen thanked him but told him that she just wanted to be left alone and get on with her life.

After Kathleen had settled back in London, Harry Jamieson, a co-worker asked her out for a meal, and she accepted, as she did like him. He was five foot nine inches tall, with dark brown hair, brown eyes and a mischievous grin. Originally from Newcastle, he was always cracking jokes with his amusing northern accent.

As Kathleen still had not heard from Colin, she took it that he did not want to keep in touch; therefore, the whole holiday romance was a farce. She missed him, however, and often thought of what would have happened if there had been no adventure or kidnap. Would she have fallen in love with him? She thought she might as well enjoy Harry's company, although she was unlikely to fall in love with him.

Harry liked Kathleen a lot. He admired her spirit and had often wanted to ask her out, but he was too shy. He was the youngest of a family of three. He had two older sisters, one, who was married and living in Bolton, and the other also married and living in Bournemouth. He was twenty-five years of age, three years older than Kathleen, but he was rather immature for his age.

They ate at a Chinese restaurant in Soho, and Harry made jokes all through dinner. Kathleen laughed, and she felt she was enjoying herself in Harry's company.

They went to a pub for a drink before departing for home. Harry had his usual pint, and she had a glass of wine. The pub was crowded, and they had to stand by the bar.

Standing in a corner with a white raincoat was a man talking to a dark haired woman. At first Kathleen thought it was Colin, and her heart missed a beat. She stared at them, and the man looked directly at her and smiled. But it was not Colin, and Kathleen turned her attention back to Harry, who was now ordering more drinks. It was Friday evening, but suddenly she felt tired and needed to go home; she mentioned to Harry that she had things to do over the weekend. The real reason was that she was hoping to hear from Colin.

Harry understood, and they drank up and left. He lived in the south of London near Clapham Junction, while Kathleen lived in the west near Holland Park. Kathleen kissed him on the cheek and told him she had a wonderful time, which she had done. They parted and went their separate ways.

Harry felt she was not ready for a relationship, but

he would keep trying. He knew in his heart that he was growing very fond of her.

Kathleen shared an apartment with a girl called Suzette, who sometimes went abroad on modelling jobs, so Kathleen hardly saw her. This suited her as she quite liked the flat to herself. She also liked her dates to be out of the apartment. She felt it was unfair to bring a man into the flat-share.

Alastair and Hermione missed Kathleen's company, but they kept in touch by telephone. John's body hadn't been found, but divers had searched the area where John had fallen into the sea.

Inspector Formby had Interpol checking out the ports of China, as well as other countries, but there did not seem to be any sign of a submarine. If he did not hear anything soon, the case would be closed. He felt sorry for Kathleen and her relatives, but the hope of finding John's body was lessening.

Chapter Sixteen

Colin was released from the hospital in Oban, a week after he had seen Kathleen. He made his way to the railway station, but before boarding his train, he telephoned Alastair for any news regarding John. Alastair had said there was no news, and Kathleen had departed for London some time ago. Alastair wished him luck, and told him to keep in touch, and perhaps keep in touch through Kathleen.

Colin arrived in London and made his way to a hotel in Bayswater. He knew that Kathleen lived near Holland Park. He was not sure of the address, but he still had her phone number. He showered and changed into clean clothes and made his way to toward her part of town, where he sat in the late sunshine looking at his mobile phone. He wondered if she would still love him, or would she become hostile towards him like when he first met her on the island. He dialled her number and waited to see if she would answer.

"Hello, who is calling, please?" a female voice asked. It did not sound like Kathleen's.

"Oh, I was hoping to speak to Kathleen. My name is Colin Edwards," he said.

"She is not here at the moment; she is working late.

Shall I tell her you called? Have you got a number she could contact you on?" asked Suzette. There was a pause.

"No. She gave me her mobile number while we were on holiday in Oban. I'm afraid I did not give her mine, as she did not ask for it," replied Colin. He quickly added. "Where does she work? I could perhaps meet her after she finishes?"

"She works in an insurance office at Holborn. Gosh, I am sorry. I cannot remember the name of it. She will be back around eight o'clock, unless she is going out to dinner with Harry," said Suzette.

"Harry, you say? I do not know a Harry. Is this a new boyfriend?" said Colin rather sharply.

Suzette paused; perhaps she was giving away too many personal details regarding Kathleen's life. "Look, I have to go now. Sorry, I was no help to you," said Suzette and she put down the phone. She knew Kathleen would not be pleased if she knew an ex-boyfriend was asking too many questions.

Colin looked at his phone, and wondered what he should do. Perhaps take the Tube into town and see if he could find her. He did not want to frighten her, but this Harry person seemed to be in the picture. He had an interview the next day at Scotland Yard, and he needed now to get himself ready for that. There was no harm in going into town for something to eat.

Colin arrived at Holborn Tube station after walking to Notting Hill Gate to catch the central line. The city was busy. People rushed here and there, and he walked along looking at buildings, looking for the name of an insurance company. He stopped at the nearest pub and ordered a pint of beer. He looked around him just in case Kathleen and that bloke Harry were there. He was beginning to get hungry, so he ordered a steak pie.

Kathleen turned off her computer, and drank the rest of her coffee, which was now rather cold. She had finished typing up a backlog of reports and decided that she would have a bite to eat nearer home. Before she left, she rang her uncle Alastair and asked how they both were and if there was any news of John. Alastair informed her that Colin had been in touch and was now somewhere in London. Had she heard from him? Kathleen told him that she had not heard from him, and anyway, she was busy at work trying to catch up with things.

Kathleen felt rather depressed. She had been asked out again by Harry, but she seemed to be constantly exhausted since her return from the island of Risskay. She felt she wanted to take things easy and day-by-day. She was cross that she had not heard from Colin. She wondered, if she did manage to see him, what her feelings would be.

Kathleen came out of the office, and made her way to the Tube station. She knew that Suzette was home and had probably eaten by now. She looked at a menu outside a pub and decided to go in. She normally did not like going into pubs by herself, but she was peckish. She managed to get a seat in an alcove and studied the menu. She ordered a glass of white wine and sausages with mash.

She noticed a man in a raincoat staring at her and wondered if he was looking at her or the woman behind her. She felt uncomfortable and tried to eat and leave as quickly as possible. She paid her bill, gathered up her belongings and left. She was sure that the man in the raincoat was following her, and she felt she needed to run. She jumped on the first train that came along, whether it was going her way or not. She looked out of the window, and saw the man looking around him.

It was late when Kathleen returned home, and she found Suzette lying on the couch watching TV. She looked up as Kathleen came in. "Why are you late and what has happened? You look as though you've seen a ghost. Have you eaten yet?" asked Suzette.

Kathleen hung up her coat and ran her fingers through her hair.

"I was followed by a man in a raincoat. I was having a bite to eat in the Black Bull pub when I first saw him, and I think he followed me to the Tube. I was so frightened! I just jumped on the nearest train, and unfortunately, it was going in the opposite direction," said Kathleen, sitting down on the couch.

"Oh, by the way, Colin Edwards phoned here early evening and wanted to speak to you," said Suzette, lighting a cigarette.

"Oh yes, Colin. I forgot about him," said Kathleen kicking off her shoes and curling into the couch.

"A boyfriend or an acquaintance?" asked Suzette puffing out smoke.

"Neither. Just good friends," said Kathleen blushing a bit. She knew Suzette was interested in her love life, which, at times, was non-existent.

Colin had a few drinks in the pub before making his way

back to his hotel. He did not see Kathleen, but he guessed that she must have made her way home by now. He would try phoning her tomorrow.

The next day Colin made his way to the glass doors of Scotland Yard and was told to sit in the waiting room.

A tall gentleman of around the age of fifty with greying hair, beard and moustache poked his head around the door and asked Colin to follow him. Colin and Mr. Neil Carmichael, as the man was called, entered a small room which looked on buildings at the rear of the Yard.

"Sit down, my fellow. I am the investigating officer, and you are hoping to join us in our investigation. The scientist case in Scotland, on the small island of Wisskay, where a submarine departed to destination unknown. I have heard that a man named Trevor escaped, while the other men on board the submarine were caught. Now this guy, Trevor, kidnapped a woman named Kathleen, the sister of John Robertson. Is that not so?" said Carmichael.

"Yes, that is right. Kathleen's kidnap was arranged by her brother, and we do not know why. Perhaps John wanted to take her away with him. There was a fight. I was knocked out and suffered a broken arm. I was later told that Trevor kicked John off the submarine, and we do not know... or should say there has been no sign of a body," said Colin.

Carmichael stroked his beard while wandering back and forth in the room thinking.

"Look, we think this guy Trevor is in London and could be dangerous. Have you managed to contact that woman Kathleen yet?" asked Carmichael.

"No, I phoned the number she gave me, but she was working late. Why? Is she in danger from Trevor?" asked Colin.

He began to feel that Kathleen was in real danger, and he had to reach her urgently. Colin phoned Kathleen's number and left a message for her to call as soon as possible, or even give him her number at work. Why was that bastard Trevor in London? Was he going to harm Kathleen? What did he really want?

Kathleen was scared that the man in the raincoat was around or near her or even spying on her. She wanted to speak to Colin as soon as possible; he would know what to do. Did she really want to see him again? She made it back to the office and answered her phone and heard a man's voice. He told her to meet him in Piccadilly Circus at three o'clock and then he rang off. Who was he? The phone rang again, but it was Suzette informing her to contact Colin, as soon as possible, as it was urgent.

Kathleen wondered how she was going to slip away from the office at that time. Could she pretend she was unwell? Suzette gave her Colin's number, and she dialled and waited.

"Hi, Kathleen, how are you; so good to speak with you," said Colin. He could not frighten her with what he had to do.

"Colin, someone called and asked me to meet him at three o'clock this afternoon in Piccadilly Circus. Am I meeting you?"

Colin knew that perhaps Trevor had found her and was going to try and kidnap her. He could hear Kathleen crying.

"Look, sweetie, I never told you to come and meet

me there. I really do not want to frighten you, but Trevor escaped from the submarine, and he is here in London. Where in Piccadilly did this man say you were to meet him?" he asked, getting more anxious.

"He never said. Someone followed me last night, but I managed to shake him off. Oh Colin, what am I to do?" Kathleen said.

"Look, I will be at Piccadilly Circus at that time; I will be standing outside the Regent Palace hotel. I will meet you there at three o'clock. I love you," said Colin and he rang off.

Kathleen could hardly eat her lunch, and she told her boss that she was feeling unwell and had to go home. She took a taxi to Piccadilly, and stood inside the Regent Palace hotel, hoping Colin would turn up soon. In fear, she looked at every man who passed her afraid he would be Trevor. She peeped outside the swing doors to look to see if Colin was anywhere near.

The traffic was dreadful. Cars honked their horns, and when Colin arrived in a taxi, he rushed into the hotel's vestibule to find Kathleen. He hurried out into the street, and he saw a woman being pushed into a car. He knew in his heart that she was being kidnapped. He tried to get the number of the black car, but it vanished into the now flowing traffic. He was sure it was Kathleen, and he dashed back to Scotland Yard to report what had happened to Mr. Carmichael. Colin wanted to see her, as he was eager to let Kathleen know that he had secured the job.

Chapter Seventeen

Kathleen had felt someone digging something into the small of her back, and she was told to move. She was bundled into a car, where she came face to face with the man in the light coloured raincoat.

"Where are you taking me? Who are you?" asked Kathleen, looking at the man. The man did not reply. He was about five foot eight inches tall, with long, lanky hair that looked like it needed a good wash. He ignored her and looked straight ahead. Oh god, she had been kidnapped again, and there had been no sign on Colin coming to her rescue.

The car drew up outside a small hotel. She craned her neck to see the name of it and the road, but she was ushered inside and taken up in the lift to the third floor. She entered a large room which looked very comfortable with a sofa, two chairs and a small table by the window with a bowl of fruit on it. She peered to see if there was another room.

"Sit down and keep quiet!" said the man in the raincoat. He went to the door and looked out and closed the door again. He ignored her, lit a cigarette and looked out of the window.

Kathleen sat looking around her; it was obvious they

were waiting for someone. Surely, Trevor had not kidnapped her. What would he want with her now? The phone went and the man answered it saying either 'yes' or 'no' before placing the receiver back on the cradle and drawing on his cigarette.

Ten minutes passed, and Kathleen began to feel very worried indeed. Nobody knew where she was, and how long was she going to be held prisoner? There were three knocks on the door, and a tall man in a cloak entered. He was smoking a cigarette held in a silver cigarette holder. He turned to face Kathleen, and said, "My dear, I apologise for this inconvenience. You must be wondering why you were brought here?" He turned around and she saw that it was Trevor. She stood up and glared at him.

She said, "Yes, for God's sake, what is going on? Why have I been brought here under armed guard?" She sat down a bit too hard and had to place her feet firmly on the ground in case the sofa fell backwards.

Trevor smiled at her, opened the drinks cabinet and helped himself to a whisky. He drank it down in one and licked his lips.

"I will tell you why. I wanted to see you again. Your dear brother John cheated me. While I was on the submarine, I found out that all the papers he had given me were false, so that I could be caught red-handed and sent to jail. I am glad I threw him off the submarine, and I hope he is now rotting in hell."

Kathleen could not bear to hear what he was saying. She stood up and came up to him. "You bastard! You killed him and all for some counterfeit papers. You did not have to throw him off the submarine; he was the only immediate family I had left. So, what do you want from me?" she asked.

Trevor smirked and took another draw from his cigarette. He said, "Quite a little wildcat you have turned out to be! In any event, I see you got safely off the island. Does your boyfriend… What is his name? Oh yes, Colin, that was it," he laughed and poured himself another drink. He continued, "I bet he does not know you are here; did you arrange to meet at the hotel? Have you seen him since you returned to London?"

Kathleen dug her nails into her hands. Trevor was teasing her and trying to find out what she knew about her brother's work. She stood up and said to him, "No, that was top secret. I never spoke to my brother about his work, and the answer to your other question is no, I have not seen or have heard from Colin." She was not being truthful, as she had heard from Colin. What a mess. She then wondered if her brother was alive, and if they were looking for him. Well, she was not going to tell Trevor anything.

"Are you hungry, my dear? I will get room service, here, look at the menu and tell us what you want," Trevor said throwing her the menu.

Kathleen sat down and looked through it. It was certainly appetising; she began to feel really hungry. She ordered melon with fruits of the forest, chicken supreme and a white coffee.

"Good, my dear. You won't mind eating in this room, do you? The dining area will be busy with tourists. In fact, I will join you, since we are getting along so well."

Trevor made the call to place the order. Twenty minutes

later, the meal was delivered on a trolley. Trevor pulled out some notes from his pocket and handed them to the waiter. Kathleen eagerly tucked into the melon.

Trevor told the man in the raincoat to go but to return at nine o'clock. Kathleen felt better that the man had left; he seemed to be threatening, and she wondered if she was going to spend the night alone.

Trevor sat opposite her, opened a bottle of white wine, and poured a little into her glass. He looked at her, smiled and remarked, "Why are you not married, a pretty woman like you?

She looked at him and said, "I never met the right guy." She then took a mouthful of melon. What was it to him if she was married or not?

He laughed and sipped his wine. "You know, I was married once; thankfully there were no children. I like to travel, see the world and do lots of interesting things. I have worked hard all my life and have done lots of training within the army and navy. That's where I learnt to navigate a ship and a submarine. I am a useful sort of guy," he said taking another sip of his wine.

"So, you go around kidnapping women?" remarked Kathleen, looking straight at him.

Trevor laughed out loud, "You are a comedian; I like your sense of humour. What have you done in your life that is exciting?" He lit up a cigarette and watched her over the smoke he had exhaled.

Kathleen started on her main course, and took another drink before answering him. "Well, if you must know, I was educated in St. Andrews at St Leonard's School for Girls.

Like my mother, I took a secretarial course so that I could get a well-paid job. My parents, unfortunately, were killed in a road accident, and so I stayed with an aunt in Edinburgh. I was very close to my brother John when we were children, but naturally we drifted apart when he went south to work. I have had boyfriends but have never found the right one to marry. I have always spent my holidays with my aunt and uncle, unless I went on holidays with girlfriends."

Kathleen suddenly felt drowsy and she felt her eyes closing. Was it the wine that she had drunk? In her confusion, she gazed down at her dinner plate, and she knew she had finished her meal. She also remembered placing two sugars into her coffee and drinking from the cup. She thought there must have been something in the coffee. After drinking it, she stood up and felt herself falling. Trevor caught her, lifted her up and carried her to the bedroom where he placed her on the bed before covering her with a blanket.

"Sweet dreams, my dear." He drank the last of his wine, put his cloak over his shoulder and let himself out quietly.

Chapter Eighteen

Colin rushed back to Scotland Yard to see Mr. Carmichael. He was sure it had been Kathleen who had been bundled into the black car, and he cursed himself for not managing to read the licence plate. He rushed through the door without knocking.

"I have just seen Kathleen being abducted, and I missed her by just a whisper. I cannot understand why someone could do such a thing, or else, let me see; of course, Trevor. Why would he want to do that to her?" asked Colin, collapsing into the nearest chair.

Carmichael looked up at Colin from the papers he had on his desk. He folded his arms and said, "My dear fellow, we are dealing with a terrorist who is wanted in many countries. He plays the game well, acting like the perfect gentleman, but he is as hard as nails. How on earth did Kathleen's brother get mixed up with him?"

Colin wiped his mouth with the back of his hand. He could lose her again. Was her brother still alive, or had he drowned when he was knocked off the submarine? He had to think hard. "Look, perhaps she is still in London; now, let's see. Where would you take her in London? A flat or a hotel? She could be out in the countryside somewhere perhaps in a barn or a farm," said Colin who now started pacing up and down the room.

"That is possible. We could, of course, start checking hotels, and we should begin with ones that are not so posh. I will get some men together and start searching as soon as possible. If she is out in the countryside, well I am sorry, you may not see her ever again," said Carmichael placing a hand on the phone. He dialled a number and played with a pen he had in his hand in readiness to take notes.

Colin was beside himself with worry. Could Kathleen's brother be alive, or did something happen between John and Trevor? One may have betrayed the other, and that was why Trevor kidnapped Kathleen in case she knew where her brother was. Why would he do a thing like that? Why could he not go away and leave Kathleen in peace? Poor lass, she had been through a lot.

Carmichael got up off his seat and suggested that they both go and have some dinner in a nearby restaurant to discuss proceedings. Colin was now beginning to feel hungry. They went into the nearest pub and sat down. They both ordered pints of beer, and Carmichael took out some papers and a newspaper. Colin took out a pen and started writing headings while Carmichael looked at the newspaper. Colin needed to think why Trevor would kidnap Kathleen. Had he fallen in love with her and kidnapped her so that he could marry her? No, that was not the case; he was being stupid now. Why did he suddenly want Kathleen? Carmichael interrupted Colin's thoughts as he told him that he had sent out at least six men to check the smaller hotels in London.

Glancing at the clock next to the bed, Kathleen saw it was ten o'clock at night. She shivered; she felt cold and was hugging the blanket which covered her. She slipped out of the bed and peered into the other room. The curtains were drawn, and the room was still in darkness. Was anyone there or was she completely alone? She moved forward quietly, just in case that man in the raincoat was sitting there waiting for her or Trevor to come back. She was alone. She moved forward to the table with the bowl of fruit on it and tucked into some grapes. She pulled the curtains back and looked out of the window. There was not much traffic, or people walking about, but there seemed to be a park or gardens across from the hotel. Which park could it be?

She looked for her coat and handbag and immediately knew it had been searched. She opened up her mobile phone to see if she could find Colin's number but her SIM card had been removed. Trevor must have done it in case she tried to call for help. She was too frightened to call the emergency services. She felt light-headed, so she made her way back to the bedroom, cuddled under the blanket and fell asleep.

Colin had an idea. He would call Kathleen's flat-mate, Suzette, and see if she could perhaps help him in the search. He dialled the number and thankfully Suzette answered.

"Hi, it's Colin again, sorry to disturb you, but Kathleen has been abducted and I was wondering if you could help me find her. She has been kidnapped by her brother's friend, Trevor. It is a long story, but could we meet for a drink, perhaps in a pub in Notting Hill Gate, if that's ok with you. Oh, by the way, what do you look like?" asked Colin.

"Kidnapped, you say. Are you sure about that? Yes, okay. I have dark red hair, and I will be wearing jeans and a green jacket. What do you look like?" asked Suzette, thinking that she may fancy Kathleen's friend, Colin.

"I am tall with brown hair and a moustache. I will be wearing a khaki raincoat. Hope to see you there," said Colin. He rang off.

Suzette ran into the bedroom, and threw some clothes onto the bed. She had just had a shower. She quickly put on some make up and clothes, and reached for her handbag and keys before rushing out of the door. This was going to be exciting, and something different from her modelling work. Poor Kathleen, she always now seemed to be in trouble ever since she returned from her holiday.

Colin saw Suzette getting out of a taxi and moved forward to greet her. She looked attractive in her outfit. She came up to him, grinning, shaking hands with him.

"Thanks for making time to meet me. What do you drink?" Colin asked taking her arm and guiding her into the packed bar.

"Oh, I will have a dry white wine. I am dying to know all about this kidnapping," said Suzette anxiously, sitting down and taking her jacket off.

Colin ordered a pint and her drink. He sat down beside Suzette and took a sip from his beer.

"When did you last see Kathleen? Was it this morning before she went to work?" he asked.

He liked the look of Suzette and wondered if she had any boyfriends.

"I saw her briefly this morning, as she was rushing off

to work. She came in rather late last night and told me that some man had followed her, but apparently she gave him the slip. She jumped on the first train, since she saw that the man on the platform was still looking for her. Strange, is it not?" Suzette sipped her wine.

"Look, I was to meet her in Piccadilly Circus at the Regent Palace Hotel, but when I got there, I saw a woman being bundled into a black car. I never got the number as it disappeared into the moving traffic. I am being helped by the Investigations Department at Scotland Yard. That is how I learnt that that bounder Trevor was in London. If only I could find Kathleen, we would know more about the situation," said Colin finishing his beer.

"What do you want me to do? I could enquire at her office if she had any strange phone calls," said Suzette. Colin got the glasses refilled, and they agreed that this was what they were going to do.

Colin said that Mr. Carmichael had organised to check all the small hotels in London, and men were stationed outside the hotels keeping watch.

They made a plan that the two of them would go as a couple and check the hotels themselves, as they might come across the one hotel where Kathleen was. It was worth a try.

Chapter Nineteen

Kathleen woke up and wondered where she was. She opened one eye and glanced at the bedside clock which said 7.30 am. The room was in darkness, and she stretched out her legs towards the bottom of the bed and yawned. She rolled over onto her side and sat up slowly. She thought she'd better see if there was anybody next door in the sitting room. She tiptoed through in case that awful man in the raincoat or even Trevor was sitting waiting for her. She nearly knocked over a chair, and she stood still waiting to see if anyone would grab her or call out. The silence and darkness were unbearable, and she pulled back the curtains to let in some light. The daylight blinded her, and she stepped back shielding her eyes. She made her way to the bathroom to freshen up. She didn't notice anything odd at first, but then she saw someone lying behind an armchair. She moved forward cautiously peering over the chair; it appeared to be the body of the man in the raincoat. Was he dead? She touched the body with her toe, but nothing happened. She put more pressure on, almost kicking it, but then noticed, to her horror, that he had been shot in the head. She had never seen a dead body before, and she stood paralysed, not daring to scream.

Had Trevor come back and killed him? Did they have a fight? She wouldn't have heard them due to the drug Trevor had sneakily put in her coffee. She ran through to the bedroom and slammed the door; her heart beating fast. From there she went to the bathroom. Sitting on the on the toilet seat, she knew had to think and recover quickly. Her first thought was to get out of there rapidly before Trevor returned and did the same to her. She opened her handbag to see if she had any make-up in it. Her hands were shaking, and she placed the bag on the edge of the bath. She found a compact and a lipstick. She looked at herself in the mirror before splashing some water on her face then applied powder and some lipstick. Luckily, Trevor hadn't taken anything else from her purse, and she had enough money to get home.

She washed and found her coat, which had been placed over a chair in the bedroom. She ran her fingers through her hair due to the absence of a hairbrush or comb and braced herself before entering the sitting room. She tiptoed towards the door, turned the handle, and to her surprise, she found it unlocked. She looked out and could not see anybody about. She slipped out, closed the door quietly behind her and moved swiftly along the passageway towards the stairs. She didn't dare to take the lift in case someone saw her and wondered what she was doing there.

Meanwhile, Colin and Suzette, pretending to be a couple, continued their visits of small hotels. They avoided the reception desk, and took it in turns to go upstairs to check the rooms without looking suspicious. They had done at least twelve hotels but had no luck in catching sight of Kathleen. It then dawned on them that Kathleen may not actually be staying at a hotel. Colin kept in touch with Carmichael by phone, informing him of their investigation so far. He enquired whether Carmichael or his men had managed to see or catch sight of Trevor, who could well be in disguise.

Now having her mobile number, Colin had tried to phone Kathleen, but obviously she was not answering, or maybe someone had broken her phone or stolen it. He was tired as he hadn't slept very well last night for worrying about Kathleen. He wished he knew where she was; this not having contact was not doing his nerves any good. Suzette was great company, however, and she bounced along beside him, placing her arm through his as to look like they were a courting couple.

Colin wondered if John was alive and out to get Trevor for trying to kill him on the submarine. Did Kathleen know that her brother could be alive? All these unanswered questions.

Carmichael phoned to say that they were at a hotel in Russell Square, and that a body, which had a gunshot to the head, had been found in one of the suites. Kathleen was not there, and the police and their forensic team were now at the scene. This was good news for Colin, as he guessed that either Kathleen had escaped or she was still being held by Trevor. He knew that she wouldn't have killed anyone, or perhaps Trevor had killed the man after fighting with him and had taken Kathleen to another location. Hopefully, they were still in London. If she had escaped, he knew that she would phone him.

Colin informed Suzette of the dead man found in the hotel room. She was horrified at the news and hoped that it wasn't Kathleen who murdered the guy.

Kathleen ran along the road. She had to get away from the hotel in case they found the body. She didn't know where Trevor had disappeared to, and she wanted to get as far away as possible from him and the hotel. She made her way to the nearest Tube station to get on a train home. Then she could phone Colin on her landline phone. She desperately needed a bath and some clean clothes.

Kathleen kept an eye out in case someone was following her. She reached the flat and as she was flustered, she rang the doorbell with the hope that Suzette was in and that Trevor didn't know where she lived. There was no answer, so she rang the next door neighbour's bell, and Mary answered sounding very sleepy indeed.

"Morning, Mary. Sorry to disturb you, but could I use your telephone? Our phone seemed to be out of order," said Kathleen.

"Why yes, of course, come on in. Would you like a tea or coffee? I was just going to make one." Kathleen nodded her head in agreement before brushing past Mary to the telephone. God, could she even remember his number? She looked into her handbag and took out the bits of paper hoping to find Colin's number.

Mary placed a steaming hot mug of coffee in front of her, added milk and two sugars.

Mary said, "Here, drink this first and then you can ring whoever you were going to phone. You look exhausted; are you okay?"

Kathleen took the mug and fell into the nearest seat. "I have this number somewhere, but for the life of me, I can't remember where," said Kathleen sipping from the mug.

Kathleen was glad she didn't have to make small talk with Mary, as Mary did most of it. How her parents were coming up to London for a few days, and George, her boyfriend, would have to move out, as her parents didn't approve of him. The cat had disappeared, and life on the whole was a bit shambolic. Kathleen nodded as though she was agreeing with her. She made some excuse and thanked Mary for the coffee.

Kathleen made her way to the nearest phone shop so that she could buy another mobile phone. She hoped to keep Trevor away from this phone so that he did not access the numbers.

Mary let Kathleen back into the flat, and in case the landline phone was bugged, she phoned Suzette's number, keeping her finger's crossed that she would answer.

On the third ring Suzette answered, "Is that you, Kathleen? Where have you been all this time? We have been worried stiff. Where are you?" asked Suzette looking directly at Colin. He took the phone from her and spoke to Kathleen.

"Hi, it's Colin, I'm with Suzette. She has been a great help in trying to find you. Where are you?"

Kathleen cleared her throat, "I managed to escape and

am at home; I discovered a body this morning after been drugged by Trevor. He must have killed that man who had kidnapped me. I am now going to take a shower, wash my hair, and change into some clean clothes."

Before she could put the phone down Colin said, "We are coming round to the house now. We have a key, so do not open the door to anyone, hear me?"

"Yes, I hear you, come quickly. I have so much to tell you."

Kathleen immediately stripped off, jumped into the shower and taking the shampoo, rubbed it into her hair. She felt unclean and she was so looking forward to seeing Colin again.

Chapter Twenty

Kathleen was still drying her hair when she heard them come in. She was standing with a towel wrapped around her body and did a quick look in the mirror. What a mess! Colin could not see her like this.

"Hello, anyone at home?" shouted Colin, throwing his raincoat onto the nearest chair.

Kathleen froze. God, they were back earlier than she thought they would be! She switched off the hair dryer and came to the bathroom door. She looked at Colin who was wandering around the lounge with his hands in his pockets. He looked up at her. She looked tired, pale and her half dried hair was hanging down her back. Kathleen felt the tears form in her eyes, as she broke down. Colin took one look at her and immediately ran over to hug her.

"There, there now. You are safe, and everything is going to be alright." He could feel her body moving closer into his. She drew back and looked at him. She noticed that he had no moustache; he must have shaved it off.

"Oh, Colin, thank god you are here. Where is Suzette?" she asked looking around the room.

"Oh, Suzette has gone to get us something to eat; hope you like Chinese?" Suzette had thoughtfully allowed Colin some time alone with Kathleen before she turned up with the carry-out. Kathleen hugged the towel closer to her body. She had not a stitch on underneath, and if the towel fell she would be embarrassed in front of him.

Colin hugged her and kissed her on the lips. He lifted her up in his arms and carried her through to the bedroom. Seeing her in a state of undress had aroused him. He laid her down on the top of the bed. She watched him, not even blinking. She knew in her heart what was coming next, and she suddenly felt herself being aroused. She watched him undress, taking off his shirt, then his trousers, leaving only his underpants. He smiled down at her, and remembered the first time he made love to her on the boat. He peeled back the towel that had covered her. She lay on top of the bed with nothing on; her full breasts waiting to be caressed. She did not say a word but just kept looking at him. He lay down beside her, smiling at her but placing a hand over her chest. He bent down and brushed his lips over her breast. He kissed her again on the lips, and this time she hugged him. He slipped his underpants off, and slipped his penis, which was aroused, into her. She made a moaning sound, as he entered her, but soon they were moving together, and both shouted out as they climaxed at the same time. Colin held her and he closed his eyes and fell asleep in her arms.

Colin and Kathleen both jumped, as they heard the front door close. How long had they been asleep?

"Go and have a shower. I will go and see to Suzette and the meal," she said throwing a towel at him. She wrapped a dressing gown around her body and brushed her hair before going into the lounge.

Suzette was in the kitchen placing the hot dishes onto plates. She looked up at Kathleen as she came in.

"Gosh, you look rather flushed; are you feeling okay?" remarked Suzette, half-smiling. She knew that Colin and Kathleen had probably made love.

"Yes, I am fine; Colin asked if he could use the shower, as he felt hot and sticky. The weather has been humid," said Kathleen feeling herself blush. Suzette was aware Colin wanted to make love to Kathleen, and Kathleen in turn had loved him, and they enjoyed their love making very much.

"Look, I bought some wine, one white and one red. I am dying for a drink," said Suzette grabbing some cutlery and moving off into the lounge.

Colin appeared dressed once again, and he smiled at both women. Kathleen suddenly felt very hungry, and she tucked into her meal, sipping her wine and smiling at Colin and Suzette. Kathleen thoroughly enjoyed the Chinese meal and discussed what they would do next.

Kathleen got dressed, and she and Colin went out to the nearest pub, which was around the corner. Suzette made an excuse that she had to make some phone calls, as she knew that Kathleen wanted to be alone with Colin.

The pub was crowded. They sat in a corner away from the door, as it was more secluded, but no one was paying attention to them.

"I want to speak to you about your brother; I have information that he could be alive," said Colin taking a sip from his beer.

Kathleen looked at him. Oh no, surely he was drowned when the submarine went down. "That cannot be true!

Why are you telling me this now?" She was beginning to be afraid. Was this the reason why Trevor had kidnapped her? Could what Colin was saying be true? She shook her head and said, "I believe what you are trying to tell me. Have you seen him?"

"Since I saw you last, I have been hired by the Investigation Department at Scotland Yard, and it is true to say that Trevor shoved John off the submarine. We now believe that John swam away and took a boat that was previously arranged for him. He has now probably arrived back in London, but where he is at the moment, we don't know, but Carmichael has fresh information on John's whereabouts."

Kathleen couldn't believe what Colin was saying to her. She placed her hand on his arm. "Why are you telling me this, Colin? I cannot believe that you came this afternoon, made love to me and then tell me the news of my brother." She didn't know if she was angry or pleased to hear this news.

Colin put an arm around her; he gave a friendly squeeze. He said, "Look, this is news to me. You know how stubborn your brother can be. He didn't mean to hurt you, but Carmichael has suggested that we can catch that villain Trevor before he does any more damage. You have got to understand that these experienced men want villains like Trevor put behind bars before they can cause more irreversible damage." He collected the glasses to get a refill of drinks.

Kathleen just sat there looking at every man in the pub to see if there was anyone like Trevor or his mates. She was glad she was with Colin but felt the last twenty-four hours was either a dream or a nightmare. She smiled at him on his return and said, "You can stay with me in the flat; I will feel safer if I am beside you. God knows, I don't want to see any other men in raincoats, not after what I experienced."

Colin said, "Your flat-mate Suzette has been a good friend to you, and she was really worried about your safety. It is best for you to stick together when you are out or going to work."

Kathleen said, "Now you really have me worried. I have just been in touch with the office, and I said that I would be back in on Monday. Nobody asked any questions, and my boss thoughtfully said that he hoped I would feel better for work by next week." Kathleen finished her drink.

They strolled out of the pub and went for a walk in Holland Park, so that Kathleen could get some fresh air. It was a sultry evening, and they sat on a bench. Colin placed an arm around her shoulders, and her head came to rest against his shoulder.

Suzette opened the door to a tall man with light fair hair with a moustache. She found him very handsome indeed and waited for him to speak.

"Good evening, my name is John Robertson, and I'm Kathleen's brother. Is she in by any chance?"

Suzette could not believe how attractive John was, so she smiled and showed him into the lounge.

"No, she is out to the pub for a drink with her boyfriend," Suzette said.

John settled himself down and drew on a lit cigarette and smiled over to Suzette, who sat opposite him.

"A boyfriend, you say? Well, good for her. It is about time she got herself one," he said looking at her. This lass was very pretty indeed, and he noticed that she didn't wear a wedding ring.

Suzette asked John if he would like a drink; she felt embarrassed sitting looking at him while he stared at her.

"Yes, that would be very nice. I will have some red wine; I see you have a bottle on the table." Suzette poured out two glasses, and as she handed one to him, she felt him touch her fingers as he took the glass.

"Kathleen will not be long; she has been quite busy at work since she returned from her holiday with her uncle and aunt." She looked at him over her glass. This was so embarrassing with him just sitting there staring at her.

"Look, I'm sorry for intruding; it is a long story to go into, but I was in the neighbourhood, and I chanced it by calling in to see her. It has been quite a long time since I last saw Kathleen. No doubt, she spoke about her holiday?" He drank the last drop of wine in his glass.

Suzette jumped up and poured some more wine into both glasses. She liked the look of him; if this was Kathleen's brother, why was he not married? She licked her lips and smiled shyly at him. If only he would stop staring at her. Should she tell Kathleen that her brother had just turned up without an invitation?

He drank his wine and stood up.

"Well, I better be off as I have things to do. Do tell Kathleen that I called. Maybe I could see you again. Perhaps a dinner date?" He raised his eyebrows with a very amused expression on his face.

Suzette clasped her hands; she did really want to see him again. "Well, that would be very nice. Just give me a ring sometime, and I will see if I am in the country. I work as a model and sometimes have to travel with the job."

John laughed and put out a hand for her to take. Suzette took his hand and shook it.

"Nice to have met you, John." He held her hand a wee bit longer, and then bent down and kissed her on the cheek.

Kathleen and Colin returned from their walk, and Kathleen noticed that the bottle of red wine was finished. Suzette could not keep a secret, and she smiled and told them that she had entertained a very handsome man called John. Kathleen stopped in her track. She asked Suzette, who the man was. "John Robertson, your brother, paid me a visit enquiring if you were in."

Kathleen fell into the armchair. So he was alive! What was her brother doing coming around to the flat? So, he definitely was in London.

Chapter Twenty-One

Kathleen could not believe that her brother was in London: she was sure that he had drowned after Trevor had pushed him into the sea. So what did he actually want? Was it to see her, or did he want something?

Colin knew she was worried, and he told Mr. Carmichael that John had turned up at Kathleen's flat.

Carmichael was interested, and he was still hoping to find Trevor before any more damage was done. He knew that Trevor was a skilful terrorist and wanted in many countries, so he needed to find him before he departed for good.

Carmichael had suggested to Colin that he should take the girls to a pub in central London and arrange for the brother to turn up as well. He then might be able to find out what exactly John wanted. So Colin suggested that to cheer up Kathleen, he would take her and Suzette to lunch in a pub beside the Thames at Westminster. Suzette was all for it, and she knew the restaurants and pubs would be busy with tourists. Kathleen smiled in her usual quiet way, never thinking that anything untoward was going to occur.

They managed to get a table beside the Thames, and so far it was a fair day with clouds and sunshine appearing through occasionally. They ordered their drinks and meals, and Colin thought it would be a good idea to let Kathleen and Suzette share a bottle of wine. He hoped that when John turned up, Kathleen would be more relaxed and not make a scene.

Mr. Carmichael had contacted John Robertson as he knew he worked for a government agency. He told him to wander down by the Thames at Westminster, where Kathleen, Colin and Suzette would be lunching. He was just to turn up casually and pretend to be surprised to see them.

John had his instructions, and he got off at a stop before Westminster at St. James' Park and walked along by the river. He knew what pub they would be in, and he made his way inside the pub, so that he could see exactly where they would be sitting. He hoped that Kathleen would not make a scene and start crying.

Kathleen was feeling quite relaxed, as she laughed at Suzette's jokes. They had nearly finished their lunch, when John appeared at their table. John smiled warmly, looked surprised and said, "Oh, I hope that I am not disturbing you. I was passing this way on this glorious day, and I looked over and there you all were." He tried to make light of the situation.

Kathleen looked up at him, and could not believe her eyes; her brother was standing not three feet away from her, although his gaze was on Suzette, who smiled back at John.

"Come and join us. We have just finished the most amazing meal and we will order you a drink," suggested Suzette, making room for him to sit beside her.

Colin watched Kathleen's reaction at her brother's

appearance. She was silent for a moment, and then John bent down and kissed her on the cheek and gave her shoulder a squeeze.

"Hi, sis, you look a bit peaky. Are you alright? I will tell you all that has happened after I get a drink." He tried to catch the waiter's attention.

Colin placed his hand on top of Kathleen's and indicated that everything would be okay. She smiled at Colin and looked across at her brother whose appearance had seemed to have changed since the last time she saw him. She said, "God, I was told you had drowned. How on earth did you manage to escape? And why did you not come back to Risskay?" She looked straight at him.

John sipped his pint of ale and smiled at her. He knew that every one of them was dying to know what happened to him. He leant back in his chair. "It is a long story. I was flung into the sea as the submarine started to dive. I noticed the boats as I frantically swam to my left side, which was north-east of the island. I managed to cling onto one of the boats which was floating near to the shore. You may not know this, but I had given Trevor false papers. I wanted him to be caught and brought to justice for all the things he'd done. However, it was arranged that a boat would come for me at nine o'clock the next morning to take me to the mainland, where I would make my way to London and the Crime Investigation Department, the CID.

"I am a scientist and work in Southampton, but I was not going to give real papers to a terrorist wanted in so many countries, before I came to Risskay to stay with aunt and uncle. I agreed to work for the CID, and they arranged false papers for me to carry on the pretence that I was going to sell them to the highest bidder in a far-off country.

"I met Trevor in London at a hotel. Here I arranged with him to organise a submarine to come to the Isle of Wisskay on a certain date, and we would travel to China to sell my G85 scientific project. I was taken by surprise when he kicked me off the submarine, but arrangements had been made that if anything unexpected happened, I was to signal for a boat to come and rescue me."

They were all leaning forward to hear what came next. Kathleen sat fascinated by her brother's story and wondered if Colin knew all about that.

"Why did you not let us know what was happening? Colin would not have had to fight for his life with a broken arm," said Kathleen rather crossly.

John looked at his sister and said, "But then you may not have met Colin, and had an adventure. I had to act the goat and not cause any suspicion. I am so sorry, I spoilt your holiday, sis. I hope I am forgiven?"

Kathleen smiled, nodded her head and said, "What's going to happen now? Did you know I was once again kidnapped? This time by a man in a shabby raincoat. I was taken to a hotel. This was arranged by Trevor, who eventually turned up, had dinner with me and then drugged my coffee. I spent the night in a hotel room not knowing that there was a dead body in the other room. I found the body the next morning, and I panicked and came home as fast as I could to be in touch with Colin and Suzette."

John looked at his watch and suggested that he would

like to invite Suzette for dinner that evening. Suzette smiled and placed a hand on John's arm.

"Why, that would be wonderful. I would love to join you for dinner."

Colin agreed that it was a wise choice; Kathleen wanted a quiet evening in. They departed in different ways, with John promising to pick up Suzette at the flat at seven that night.

Kathleen was tired when she returned to the flat. She wondered if it was the wine that made her sleepy or the excitement of meeting her brother, who'd come back from the dead. He certainly had changed his appearance, and she agreed that he looked very handsome.

Chapter Twenty-Two

A couple of weeks passed and Kathleen saw more of her brother. Colin and John seemed to be working for the CID in trying to locate Trevor. Their department was anxious to find Trevor before he left the country. They knew that he was still in the UK, as there had been sightings.

John and Colin were given information that Trevor was near the Thames. A group of men from CID including John and Colin set off toward Tower Bridge. They watched a group of men on a platform by the river. They were all waiting for something to happen or perhaps meeting someone. Suddenly a motorboat approached the platform with three men on board. They landed, and the tallest of the group who was dressed in a cloak, dark glasses, and smoked a cigarette, stepped forward and shook hands with the group of men.

They spoke a few words and a package was passed to the tall man. Immediately John identified Trevor dressed in the cloak. He whispered to Colin and nodded to the CID group of men.

Trevor shook hands with the group on the platform, returned to the boat and set off towards Kew Gardens. John spoke into his mobile phone giving instructions. The men on the platform started to move away from the river but turned to watch a motor launch speeding towards them. Another motor launch was speeding down the Thames towards Kew Gardens to intercept Trevor. The two motor launches were from the police who were awaiting instructions to advance to the platform and arrest the group, while the other one gave chase down the Thames towards Kew Gardens.

The police landed on the platform keeping low as a group of men started to run turning to fire at the police. One of the men fell holding onto his stomach, as the other men tried to escape. John and Colin approached the group cautiously cutting off any escape at Tower Bridge. John was wounded in his shoulder, and he dropped his gun. He placed his hand on his shoulder to stop the bleeding and to relieve the pain. Colin picked up his gun and fired over the heads of the small group who were being handcuffed. Two police launches were in tow after Trevor's boat. Trevor fired at one of the launches who returned fire. The other police boat circled the other boat so that he would either crash or stop.

Trevor was still firing at the police boats when a bullet hit his shoulder. He placed his hand on his wound falling onto the boats deck. The two police boats slowly pulled up to besides Trevor's boat. They pointed their guns at him, holding onto his shoulder. He looked up and spat out, "You bastards!"

The police took no notice and roughly heaved him up to a standing position. One of the policemen that appeared to be in charge said to Trevor, "You are under arrest for espionage and drug trafficking in many countries." He shoved Trevor off the boat and up the platform where several of the bodies were being removed. Trevor came face to face with John who looked quite happy to see Trevor arrested. He then looked at John, and before the police moved him on, he said, "I should have killed you on that island when I had the chance."

Chapter Twenty-Three

Kathleen opened her eyes and found Colin looking at her. He was lying on his side, leaning on one elbow. He smiled and said to her, "You look beautiful when you sleep and look so peaceful."

Kathleen grunted. She thought was he trying to butter her up after the excitement of the battle between the policemen, John and Colin. She smiled and placed her hand over his face. Colin caught her hand and kissed it. They gazed at one another before Kathleen spoke, "Did Suzette accompany John to the hospital to get his shoulder seen to? She certainly likes my brother very much, and I know he is keen on her as well."

Colin smiled and lay on his back looking up at the ceiling. He took Kathleen in his arms and kissed her on the lips. She responded by placing one leg over his body, and manoeuvring herself on top of him. She smiled down at him, pushing her body closer to him and smiling all the time. Colin rolled her over, so that he was on top of her, and he smiled and kissed her again on the lips. He knew that she wanted him to make love to her.

Suzette sat beside John as the doctor looked at his shoulder. The doctor looked serious, and he took out a needle and placed it into John's arm so that he wouldn't feel the bullet being removed. A nurse was standing by. Suzette squeezed John's hand to help him relax.

"God, I hope I am a better patient than Kathleen," said John looking at Suzette, who looked pale and tired after the fighting episode. He was glad she had insisted on coming to the hospital with him.

"Well now, that will probably hurt for a few days, but I would like to see you again in a week's time." Turning to Suzette the doctor said, "Young lady, look after your man, and see that he has plenty of rest."

Suzette smiled.

"You bet I will; I'm not going to let him out of my sight."

John laughed and hugged her.

Kathleen cooked bacon, eggs and tomato for breakfast, while Colin made some toast and hot drinks. She was hungry, and after all she'd been through on the island, and in London, she was so glad Colin was with her. She could not bear to be separated from him.

Colin glanced over at her, and thought himself a very lucky fellow, as both of them had come a long way since they had met in London and on the island of Risskay.

Kathleen returned to work, as she had a lot of catching up to do. Her boss was pleased to see her, but did not ask too many questions. It had been an exciting few days, and she was glad that Suzette and John had become good friends. John had never really told her of his private life, and she never dared to interfere. They were a bit private in their lives, and Kathleen always considered her brother a scholar, who never really had many girlfriends. Kathleen never really had many boyfriends, so she couldn't talk.

Harry Jamieson was pleased to see her back at work, although he was now dating one of the typists, a girl called Caroline. Caroline had long blonde hair, green eyes, and a pout. They seemed to be happy together, and Kathleen told him that she was pleased for him. Kathleen also told him she was dating a wonderful man, whom she had met on holiday.

Colin and John, who had recovered well from his little operation on his shoulder, were congratulated by Carmichael and his team. John was told that Trevor would go on trial and receive a very lengthy prison sentence. John had done a splendid job on the Scottish islands and in London. Carmichael also apologised for dragging his sister Kathleen into the operation, but both girls had done well.

John and Colin went to the nearest pub to celebrate. Colin wanted to speak to him about Kathleen, as he wanted John's permission to marry Kathleen. Colin hoped that Kathleen, who had been willing to make love and enjoy his company, would accept his proposal. John laughed and slapped Colin in a friendly manner. He said that he would be glad that someone would marry his sister, and he wished good luck to them both.

Colin took Kathleen out to a restaurant in the centre of London, and waited for the right moment to propose to her. They made small talk throughout the meal, and afterwards, they strolled by the river and stood on Westminster Bridge looking out towards Tower Bridge. Colin placed his arm around Kathleen and said, "Kathleen, I love you, and always will love you. I know you have had a bad time this summer, but I have asked John for your hand in marriage. He has agreed to the marriage, as it is your happiness and welfare he cares about. Will you be my wife?"

Kathleen looked at Colin. She asked herself if she wanted to marry him. He was always there for her and even when it was dangerous. She had grown to love him. She held his hand and said, "Oh, Colin, what can I say? I have only known you for such a short time, but you were always there for me, through thick and thin, and I am sorry I was rude to you when we met on the Isle of Risskay. I have grown first to like you and now have fallen in love with you. In my heart, I have this deep feeling that I will always love you. Yes, I will marry you."

Colin hugged her and kissed her hard. "You have made me a very happy man, and I will take care of you, as I love you so much."

They returned to the apartment hand in hand.

John was lying on the couch with Suzette curled beside him. He stroked her hair and wondered if Colin had proposed to Kathleen yet. He thought of marriage himself, perhaps to Suzette, as she would make a good wife. No, not yet; it was far too soon. Suzette looked up at him, and wondered if she was really in love with John. He was strong and had a strong nature. He did not like to be bossed about and preferred to be always in control.

Colin and Kathleen turned up looking happy, and still with their arms around each other, they announced that they were engaged. John opened a bottle of champagne he had bought earlier in preparation of the good news.

They sat around discussing where they would get married. Kathleen jokingly mentioned the Isle of Wisskay, but who would want to go there after all that had happened? It was decided that it should be a Register Office in London, and the marriage would take place in the autumn.

Uncle Alastair and Auntie Hermione could come over for the wedding, since it would be before the bad weather hit the islands. They had been informed that John had been rescued, and Trevor was up for trial and sentencing.

Colin wanted to get married as soon as he could, as he did not think it was fair to Kathleen to keep her waiting too long. He also didn't want to give her time to change her mind.

On the 5th of October 2000, Kathleen and Colin were married with John as best man and Suzette as maid of honour. Alastair and Hermione were over the moon that Kathleen was at last a bride, and they all hoped that Colin and Kathleen would be very happy in the years to come.

The Reluctant Bridegroom

Chapter One

The sunshine nearly blinded her as she drew back the bedroom curtains. She opened the window and gazed at the brilliant colours adorning her garden.

Veronica Wyllie was a woman in her fifties, small, dark haired with patches of grey beginning to show at the sides of her short hair. She had just come down from London to the small village of Hearsley where she hoped to retire and end her days.

Her husband Larry had passed away six years ago with a fatal heart attack, and her only daughter, Susan, was married and living in Auckland, New Zealand.

Veronica had taken early retirement, and after some months of looking at different houses and flats, she fell in love with Bluebell Cottage in this small quaint village.

She drew on her dressing gown and made her way down the stairs to the kitchen to make herself some toast and tea for breakfast. It was Saturday, and she had been at the cottage for nearly a week after the great upheaval of moving from London.

The occupants of the village were very friendly but were inclined to keep to themselves as they were not too sure of strangers.

Mrs. Jean Docherty, a widow in her late sixties, lived next door on the right and was a very keen golfer. Her husband had died nearly ten years ago and her family were scattered around the country.

The Hutchison's on the other side of her were also very pleasant, but Mrs. Hutchison loved to gossip and was inclined to boss her poor husband, Fred around. He was in his early seventies and was a retired bank manager. Doris Hutchison was a very large lady and loved to bake for the local Women's Rural Institute (WRI).

Veronica had dated a widower for nearly four years in London, but he had become very possessive. The last time she visited his two daughters, they appeared quite hostile towards her, so she was thankful she had escaped that relationship.

It was nearly the end of September that year when she received an invitation to attend the golf club's annual dinner/ dance. They always held this on the first of October every year and the whole village turned out for the occasion.

On Saturday evening, 1st October,1989, Veronica put on an emerald green blouse and a long black skirt and wore very high court shoes to help her appear taller. The gentlemen she had met since arriving at Hearsley were retired or young farm labourers, but of course she was not looking for romance. Well, not yet.

The golf club was packed with various age groups and she accompanied Jean Docherty and the Hutchison's who had given them a lift to the event.

Veronica loved dancing and she remembered how she and Larry twirled around the dance floor dancing a quickstep as her feet hardly touched the ground. Oh, what memories.

The meal finished quickly, the dancing commenced, and she knew she was going to be frustrated to sit while watching the dancers float around the room.

A very tall, immaculately dressed gentleman appeared to ask her for the next dance.

He was six feet three inches tall, handsome with a Ronald Coleman moustache. His hair was receding and was starting to go grey. His aftershave smelt of Old Spice, not one of Veronica's favourites.

His name was Stephen Henderson, and he was a very successful but semi-retired surgeon in London. He had three grown-up children. One was married and living in Toronto, Canada while the single ones lived in London. He had been married and divorced twice.

Mrs. Hutchison informed her that he was extremely clever, very wealthy and even owned a villa in the South of France among his other properties. He owned the local golf club, the local hotel and lived in the big mansion overlooking the golf course; otherwise, he spent his time in London living it up in clubs, etc.

A month passed since the dinner/dance, and the dark evenings were now drawing in. Veronica spent her time tidying up the garden before winter approached and the night frosts set in. She wished she could spend Christmas with her family, but it would have been impossible to go to New Zealand, since she had bought her property.

The telephone rang one evening, and to her surprise it was the dashing Stephen Henderson. He invited her to meet him for a coffee and a chat at the Royal Hotel on Saturday at 7.30 p.m. Veronica took this to be only drinks and not a meal, so she informed him she would take a taxi to the hotel.

She had not given Stephen a thought since the dance and was surprised that he had called her. What was he up to?

Saturday evening arrived very quickly. She decided to wear the red dress she bought in the London summer sales which definitely accentuated her slim figure.

The taxi arrived on time and as it was raining she put on her black raincoat. She had two gin and tonics before she left the house and indeed spent most of her time running to the loo. Was it nerves at meeting him again, or was she excited to be asked to go and meet with him again? She arrived at the hotel and she made straight to the ladies to powder her nose, making sure she looked presentable.

He was standing in reception looking around him, and she paused for a moment before greeting him. He shook her hand and placed it through his arm as they made their way to the cocktail bar. They made polite conversation talking about their lives, ex-wives, her husband and families. Veronica stuck to gin and tonic while he drank a few whiskies.

The time flew and she kept thinking that she must order a taxi to take her home as it was now 10 p.m. He explained his work at the hospital of St. Thomas's in London and before she knew it was 10.30 p.m. He insisted he would see her home as he was going back to Hearsley that evening.

He drove her back safe and sound before pulling up beside

her door, but Veronica knew that Doris Hutchison would probably be looking out of her window as she usually did. He bent over towards her, and for a moment she thought he was going to kiss her. At the last moment, she turned to look at him thanking him at the same time, he kissed her on the cheek, informing her that he had a wonderful evening and that she was great company. She opened the car door feeling a wee bit embarrassed. He promised to call her again quite soon, and she replied she would look forward to his call.

Chapter Two

Weeks passed and Veronica never heard from the dashing Stephen Henderson. Christmas arrived and she invited her best friend Phyllis Johnston from London to spend the festive season with her.

Phyllis was a friend Veronica had made when she worked for the First National City Bank of New York in London. Phyllis was a telephonist and Veronica was an audio typist for two bosses, one in the Corporate Division and the other in the Credit Control Department. The work was pretty boring, but the staff were great fun.

Phyllis was tall and slender with black hair worn on top of her head in a bun. She had done some part-time modelling for a magazine in her spare time, but she continued to work at the bank. Veronica remembered her days at the office and especially about Jeannie, the filing clerk, who wore very short skirts. She was always showing off a bit of leg to the boys, and she had damn good legs too.

Phyllis left on the 29th December, 1989 after staying for four days at Veronica's. She was going to spend New Year's Eve in Scotland with friends. Veronica missed her company but was invited by her neighbours, the Hutchison's, for supper on the 1st January, 1990.

On the evening of the 29th December she received a phone call from Stephen Henderson. He was asking her to join him for lunch on the 31st December in Guildford, the nearest big town to Hearsely. She was very surprised to hear from him and wondered why he was phoning her. He had flu over Christmas up in London and was planning to spend New Year's Eve in Hearsley. He was as charming as ever on the phone and apologized for not keeping in touch with her.

Veronica did some last minute shopping before the New Year, buying some wine and Madeira. She had invited the neighbours next door for drinks before the bells at midnight on 31st December, 1989.

Once again she ordered a taxi to take her to Guildford to the Regency Hotel. She had chosen a midnight blue dress and wore a string of pearls around her neck. She was not too sure if she really wanted to see Stephen again, but she loved going out. She also realised that she had to make an effort to meet people.

He was waiting for her in the car park beside his Aston Martin and handed her a large bouquet of flowers. Of course, she was delighted, and they made their way into the busy hotel restaurant. Veronica wanted to take this relationship rather slowly. Most of the men she had been out with were not as generous as Stephen, and she often had to pay her way with the promise of a next meeting. Often, she had never heard from them again.

Time seemed to fly as they talked on various subjects. Veronica felt relaxed and chatted away to him. She knew he was a good looking man yet somehow she wasn't that drawn to him, but Stephen had told her that he found her a very attractive lady. She was glamorous, had a good dress sense, but sometimes she gave the impression of being shy and sensitive. They finished their meal after spending two hours, and it was now 3.30 p.m. He asked her to come for coffee in a few days' time at his house in Hearsley, and he would be in touch with her.

New Year's Eve was quiet around the village, as most people retired early and went to bed. The Hutchisons arrived at five minutes to midnight on the 31st December. Fred had a whisky while Doris and Veronica sipped medium dry white wine when the New Year arrived. Jean from next door arrived five minutes later, and they all celebrated for a couple of hours drinking and talking while soft, romantic music played in the background.

The next day, the telephone woke Veronica at 10.00 a.m. She was surprised that it was Stephen calling to wish her a happy new year for 1990. He was inviting her for coffee on the 4th January, 1990, at 2.30 p.m. at his house, after all the festive season was still going strong. She thanked him for the lunch and flowers and wished him a happy new year and was looking forward to seeing him.

Chapter Three

After celebrating New Year's, the 4th of January came very quickly.

There was no snow on the ground but the weather was sunny and frosty. In fact, there appeared to be more sun that winter than the previous summer.

Veronica's neighbours knew by now that she was being courted by Stephen Henderson. They wished her well, but they warned her to be careful and not to be taken in by his small talk and money. Veronica had never been a social climber. She treated everyone just the same. She was never money conscious and was very grateful that Larry had left her comfortably off.

She had decided that, as it was such a glorious day, she would walk to the mansion house. She dressed casually in green slacks, brightly coloured jumper, boots, a hat to keep her head warm and a warm black jacket.

Stephen's mansion was certainly imposing with its long drive and well-cut lawns.

She had brought a gift of a bottle of malt whisky. She felt very guilty in not giving him a Christmas present.

Stephen opened the door welcoming her into the living room where a large log fire was burning in the hearth. A black Labrador raised its head in a greeting and returned to sleep.

She settled on one of the sofas near the fire and accepted a glass of sherry as a New Year drink. They talked about how they spent New Year's Eve, and of course he had been up in London visiting his family, Christopher and Rachel.

Veronica listened intently. She was known as a very good listener and nodded in agreement where it was appropriate. She once tried to tell him about her daughter living in New Zealand, but she found he was not really all that interested.

The New Year flew in very quickly, and by the end of January, she still hadn't heard from Stephen Henderson.

Veronica decided to visit friends in London. Although she preferred the countryside to the hustle and bustle of London, she did miss seeing the different shops.

Phyllis, her friend, visited Veronica in early February, for a few days and they went to London to do some shopping and to visit the theatre. Veronica enjoyed the theatre, and they managed to see *Cats* and *Les Miserables,* as well as shopping at the sales.

On the 10th February, an invitation arrived from Stephen Henderson a Valentine's cocktail party at his house on the 14th February, 6 p.m. to 8 p.m. The majority of Hearsley would be attending, especially the golfers. Veronica was not surprised at receiving the invitation. She was beginning to get used to hearing from him only now and again. It was obvious to her that he wanted to be friends and nothing more, but he was always all over her when they met, so perhaps he was like that with all his lady friends.

Phyllis was still at Bluebell cottage, so Veronica rang

to ask if she could bring a friend to the party. She really wanted Phyllis to meet Stephen and to see what she thought of him.

On Valentine's Day, Veronica received a large bouquet of flowers from Stephen, informing her that he really did miss her and was so looking forward to seeing her again.

The house was packed with lots of guests mostly from the medical world and London. The champagne flowed freely at the beginning of the evening, and Veronica and Phyllis mingled with the local Hearsley crowd.

They were both weary from standing and at 7.45 p.m. were glad that the evening was drawing to a close. Veronica hardly saw Stephen. He was too busy floating from guest to guest and being the charming host. She really did wonder why she had been asked to the party.

They were about to leave when Stephen insisted that they must stay for supper. Veronica gave in and she hoped she would be alone with him later on. There were around ten people around the dinner table including his son and daughter. Veronica knew instantly that Rachel, the daughter, did not like her. Christopher was tall with fair hair and good looking like his mother and Rachel, the daughter, was dark like her father, and personality-wise was probably was like one of Stephen's other wives.

Stephen sat at the head of the table beside a professor and his wife. Veronica and Phyllis were placed beside a tall, fair haired man named Dr. Michael Owen. He was very polite and listened intently to what the two women had to say. Veronica relaxed, began to enjoy herself, and felt physically attracted to him.

Although he kept talking to his guests, Stephen kept glancing at Veronica. Meanwhile, Phyllis became a wee bit tipsy and occasionally broke into a loud laugh. She was certainly enjoying herself. Veronica found out that Dr. Michael Owen worked with Stephen at the hospital and were great friends. His wife had been killed in a car crash some years before, and since his children were all grown up, he lived alone in Redhill.

They departed after eleven o'clock with Dr. Michael Owen giving them a lift back to Bluebell Cottage.

Phyllis thought Stephen Henderson was very handsome and full of confidence, but she was concerned that one should never double-cross him because one would live to regret it. This remark made Veronica shiver and she knew she had to be careful. Phyllis never mentioned Dr. Michael Owen and Veronica was glad, as she liked him a lot.

Chapter Four

February passed and the cool March days became brighter as spring approached.

Veronica had started to date Stephen Henderson seriously, and indeed the relationship became more romantic as they grew closer and got to know each other. He had invited her to dinner at his house and she had reciprocated. There were many visits to London enjoying concerts, shows, etc. and indeed their relationship began to blossom. At the beginning of August, he proposed marriage to her.

Veronica was surprised and wondered if she was really ready for this so soon. For Stephen, once his mind had been made up, there was no going back. He had swept her off her feet and took her to London to choose a very expensive engagement ring. She chose a ring with four diamonds while not really paying attention to the price tag of over three thousand pounds. She felt very guilty at choosing such an expensive ring, but Stephen seemed delighted and later took her to the Ritz Hotel for lunch.

Hearsley was full of gossip and the women were envious of Veronica's ring. She knew she was the talk of the village, but she was happy and did not care. In September they flew to Paris for a romantic weekend taking in the sights and enjoying a trip down the river. She had always been very independent and insisted on paying her way or at least the airfare. Stephen would not hear of it. He remarked that they came into this world without money and when they died they couldn't take it with them.

Veronica felt uncomfortable about this arrangement, as after all, she was only engaged to him and not married. She did find it infuriating when he got cross when she insisted on paying for some of the meals. He would make a remark that she wanted to be an independent woman.

The weeks flew by and she found herself spending more time at his house in Hearsley. They now had regular sex and Veronica found it hard to climax. He always came before her, and she was left rather frustrated.

Veronica and Stephen were now engaged for over a year, and it was becoming quite embarrassing for her because folk kept asking when were they getting married. She would make some feeble excuse and remark that they had not set a date. In the end, people got fed up of asking her. She still lived at Bluebell Cottage as if nothing mattered. She had been to his villa in the South of France several times and had a wonderful time swimming, sunbathing, sightseeing and relaxing. She noticed that he was a very different person on holiday away from the pressures of work and his daughter, Rachel, who always seemed to nag him. Veronica knew that Rachel did not like her and indeed did not approve of the engagement, and this was probably the reason she could never get him to set a wedding date. He kept putting it off for another year.

In the year 1992, while shopping in Harrods at the January Sales and thinking she could spend an entire day browsing, as there was so much to see, she bumped into Dr. Michael Owen in the Food Hall. He was just the same as the last time she had seen him at the cocktail party. As it was so busy they made their way to Fortnum and Mason for tea.

Veronica compared the two men and found that the Michael appeared to be a very quiet man who never raised his voice. Stephen had a temper and would be inclined to sulk if he did not get his own way. This made the atmosphere electric.

Dr. Michael Owen seemed pleased to see her and asked how Stephen was keeping. This came as a surprise to her, as she knew they worked together in hospital. He told her they had an argument and Stephen had taken the huff and had not apologized. They continued talking for ages. Veronica knew that this man was very attractive, and she was beginning to wonder if she was truly in love with Stephen Henderson.

Seven months later, Stephen held a garden party for friends. Veronica was glad that Dr. Michael Owen was invited. It was at this time she noticed him staring at her as if he was watching her every move.

Stephen was so wrapped in his work that he never noticed the growing relationship between Veronica and Dr. Michael Owen. Anyway, he was staying up in London more often.

Veronica plucked up courage and asked Michael over for dinner at Bluebell Cottage while Stephen was away in London. She cooked roast lamb followed by crème brulee, coffee and mints. She was nervous to begin with but soon relaxed with the help of the white wine they had at dinner. He was so different to Stephen, and they cuddled up together on the couch. He kissed her gently on the lips, and she melted into his arms. She felt sixteen again and never wanted the evening to end.

Chapter Five

Veronica never felt very guilty in her relationship with the doctor, and she knew that one day she would have to inform Stephen about this relationship with his friend Michael. She also knew that Rachel would be over the moon if she broke off the engagement to Stephen. His other children did not seem to mind as their priority was to see their father happy.

October, 1992, was a wonderful month for Veronica. She had been seeing a lot of Dr. Michael Owen and they had spent several weekends away in different parts of England. He spoilt her by giving her gifts of anything she wanted or saw in the shops.

Stephen guessed that Michael was frequently seeing Veronica and knew that they were lovers. He kept his distance for the moment and hoped she would make up her mind which man she wanted as a husband.

Christmas 1992 came and Dr. Michael Owen bought her a cashmere cape for Christmas and she wore it to show off in front of the neighbours. She remembered all the chocolates and flowers Stephen had showered on her over the years, but he never really asked her what she really wanted for Christmas or for her birthday. She had tried to tell Stephen several times about her relationship with the doctor, but he never really listened to her.

Veronica remained living in Bluebell Cottage and refused Stephen's invitation to stay at his house. She prayed that this relationship would work out with Dr. Michael Owen.

Phyllis stayed with Veronica on New Year's Eve, and Dr Michael Owen kept a discreet distance.

Stephen did not break off the engagement, and Veronica felt very trapped. She knew he only wanted a pretty woman on his arm and sex. She knew she could not give that to him now. Stephen was always very charming in front of family and friends. He pretended that the relationship was blooming, and Veronica noticed that Dr. Michael Owen was now never invited to his house. She missed him a lot at the parties. She liked Stephen very much, but she knew she was not in love with him and never was in the first place.

Spring 1993 came in with a blaze of colour. The birds started building their nests and Veronica always made sure there was plenty of water in the birdbath. The garden looked good after the winter, and she was proud of her little cottage. The neighbours next door were still very friendly, and sometimes Veronica would bake some scones and cakes to help Doris's WRI parties. She would also play a round of golf with Jean, and Stephen would ask her now and again for dinner acting as if nothing had ever happened. Veronica always tried to explain that his family did not approve of their engagement, but Stephen would laugh away the whole situation.

Veronica decided that she needed a holiday, so she arranged with Phyllis to go abroad in May when it was not too hot. They booked to go to Majorca; it was a long time since they visited that island. Veronica was not one for sunbathing on a beach, she liked to go sight-seeing preferring to visit cathedrals, museums and palaces. She also enjoyed sailing and looked forward to a cruise down the coast.

Phyllis always packed far too many clothes and then was worried about the weight of her suitcase. She had been married when she was seventeen, but after a tragic miscarriage, her husband left her for another woman, and she never really got over it. She married again and had a son, but after ten years of marriage, her husband suddenly died of a heart attack. Her son, once he reached the age of nineteen, never kept in touch.

Stephen had been rather jealous of her going away on holiday without him. He was worried that the two of them would meet some male companions and have sex with them. He had lectured her before she went away and became very jealous and possessive. He raised his voice and accused her of meeting male friends while visiting London. Veronica was not amused. She hated being accused of something she had not done, and she knew she had her doubts about marrying him. She hated jealous and possessive men, so she made up her mind; she was going on holiday whether he liked it or not.

The week in Majorca went well. The weather was warm and sunny. They did have one or two rainy days, but that did not put them off going places. They toured the island, swam in the hotel pool and in the sea. At the end of the holiday, she was sorry to return to rainy old Britain. Stephen met them at Gatwick airport and drove them back to Bluebell Cottage.

Jean, Doris and Fred were glad she was back. They spent the next day telling her the village's gossip. Apparently, although they didn't want to upset Veronica, Stephen was seen out with a lady at the local hotel. Veronica listened quietly, as this was something she was good at. She knew she had to make her mind up about the two men. So was it to be Stephen or Michael?

Stephen did not mention anything to her about a lady friend. She did not say anything about it, but accepted an invitation to dinner.

He had invited her the following Friday and they had a pleasant meal with good conversation and wine. They had coffee in the lounge looking on to the terrace and beautiful gardens.

Veronica waited for him to take his usual after dinner cigar before mentioning the subject of the 'lady friend'. He took a drag from his cigar screwing up his eyes through the smoke. They looked at one another, and Veronica knew that he had something to tell her.

Chapter Six

Veronica was not at all surprised to hear from Stephen that he was dating a lady doctor from the hospital. The rumours had been true, and she suddenly felt that there was nothing, not even jealousy, and from that moment, she knew in her heart she had never been in love with him. She had to speak the truth now, and it was best that they should move on with their lives and not get married.

Stephen did not appear to be surprised at her decision and was quite relieved. They both felt free. To her surprise, he was as nice as pie to her and there wasn't a shouting match. She took the ring off her finger and gave it back to him. When she got to the front door, he hugged her close and told her he hoped that they would remain friends. He opened the palm of his hand revealing the ring, and put it into her hand insisting that she must keep it. He wished her all the best with her new man, Dr. Michael Owen.

The months flew by and Veronica settled back in to her life once again at Bluebell Cottage. She threw all her energy into gardening and visiting friends.

Dr. Michael Owen was not at all surprised at the break-up of the engagement, and he stayed away purposely so she could sort out her life. He would return to court her, and when she was ready, he would ask her to marry him.

After three months, Dr. Michael Owen started to call round, and often he would stay at Bluebell Cottage, or she would stay at his house in Redhill, Surrey. He still worked at the hospital and quite often she would not see him for days. He was a busy man.

Early in January 1994, Dr. Michael Owen proposed marriage to her and she accepted. They got married later that year in Hearsely's parish church and had the reception at the local hotel. Stephen gave her away.

Stephen Henderson's relationship with his lady doctor had ended after six months, just after Veronica was engaged to Michael. He had a few lady friends, but it looked like he was not going to get married.

Veronica sold Bluebell Cottage and moved to Redhill from where she often went to London by train. After three years, they went to New Zealand on holiday to visit her daughter. They promised themselves that when Michael retired they would travel around the world.

Veronica never felt better or happier, and she knew in her heart that she had married the right man.

They often went to visit Stephen, but he never married but continued living and enjoying life to the full. His son, and daughter, Rachel, married respective partners and were living abroad in Australia and America. Stephen retired and lived in Hearsley, lording over the village and the golf club.

Poor Fred died very suddenly of a heart attack. Jean and Doris became the best of friends.